The
Instructor

Also by Ann Ireland

A Certain Mr. Takahashi

The
Instructor

ANN IRELAND

THE ECCO PRESS

THE ECCO PRESS
100 West Broad Street
Hopewell, New Jersey 08525

Printed in the United States of America

Library of Congress Cataloging-in-Publication Data

Ireland, Ann.
 The instructor: a novel / by Ann Ireland.
  p. cm.
 ISBN 0-88001-537-3
 I. Title.
PR9199.3.I68I57   1997
813'.54—dc20   96-43003

Designed by Heather Hodgins

9 8 7 6 5 4 3 2 1

FIRST EDITION

For Tim, Tom, and my folks.

ACKNOWLEDGMENTS

The author thanks the Toronto Arts Council and the Ontario Arts Council for their financial aid during the making of this book.

For sympathetic readings and editorial advice, thanks to the following people: Cynthia Holz, Tim Deverell, Audrey Thomas, Bill Deverell, Tekla Deverell, Tamara Deverell, Ellen Seligman, Deepa Mehta, and especially Jenny Munro who read the manuscript many times.

At Doubleday Canada, big thanks to *The Instructor*'s editor, Alison Maclean.

A man or woman sunk in dreams that cannot be spoken, about a life they do not possess, comes suddenly to a door in the wall. They open it. Beyond the door is that life and a man or woman to whom it is already natural ... the secret life is suddenly revealed.

Jeanette Winterson, *Sexing the Cherry*, 1989

PROLOGUE

THE BOY WOULDN'T stand still. He kept dancing in and out of focus, blurring his own edges as he tossed off his clothes. First a red baseball hat flew to the ground, then the denim vest, the T-shirt, and finally his high-top sneakers. He was a compact boy, not gangly and stumbling over himself like some.

"Around here they quit growing early," Father liked to say. Meaning not just their bodies.

He took a step forward through the dry grass of the escarpment until his toes hugged the edge of the cliff. There he stood still for an instant, eyeing the waves below, choosing his moment. His thigh muscles sprang into firm ridges. If such an action made a sound it would be a sharp elastic ping. Sweat trailed down his back, ducking toward the hollow part at the base of his spine. Here it would be slippery and cold, and here, I decided, adjusting the focus of the binoculars, was the most perfect part of his body; this tiny patch of skin where it sank into the waist of his shorts. This was a place a girlfriend might graze her cheek, run her tongue along, and feel him shiver.

PART ONE

1

MY DEAR OTTO:

See my hand shaking like crazy? It's not because I'm scared, not in the least. Though two hours ago I was so damn nervous and fidgety I scurried to the outhouse every ten minutes, then worried you'd choose that instant to roll up the hill. There I'd be, popping open the door of the little pagoda, while you leaned against the door of your car, grinning.

I jammed crackers in my mouth, thinking I needed the salt.

Why was I in such a state?

After all, you were history.

The phone call had come out of the blue. "Let's have tea, just the two of us," you said, your voice so low and intimate I glanced over my shoulder just to make sure you weren't standing there.

My own voice, when it found itself, was guarded. "Late afternoon is best. I've got meetings."

That sounded important.

It is important. We're running through the slate for next year's program and I've been fighting for that New Music trio to be given the residence position.

"Why do you want —" I said, too late, into the dead phone. As was your habit, you'd hung up without warning. I was shaking then too ... for this was my chance to show you what I'd become, how I'd devised a life of my own.

To begin with, the vehicle was all wrong. Come on, Otto, a brick-colored Honda? It had to be a rental.

When you slipped out of the car, legs first like some starlet, I let out a sigh. For it was you, in the flesh and life-size. You strolled up the dirt path jiggedy-jog, legs bent at the knees, hands thrust deep into your pockets, so loose-limbed I swore you were about to keel over. Your face, grinning widely, so sure of its welcome, grew bigger and bigger — and still I didn't move a muscle. I was nailed to the position I'd decided on since yesterday's phone call: arms crossed, back sloped against the doorjamb of the cabin, wearing a black tank top that bled into the darkened interior. Like some Walker Evans photo, I decided, most of my hair drawn back with an elastic, the rest sweeping over my face in the lake breeze.

"Very nice, Simone," you nodded, missing nothing. A cigarette dangled from your lips. I let you come right up until our toes touched.

"Hello, Otto."

Of course we embraced, though perhaps a little stiffly. My face got buried in the base of your neck and it seemed to me I'd spent a lot of time gazing into the hollow of your throat where the pulse tapped silently. My fingers curled around the cloth of your collar — threadbare, soft denim — and I was whisked without warning to that hill outside San Patricio: hard earth and scrubby cactus, burros grazing. The heat and dryness made our skin crack and fissure, mimicking the landscape. We'd hiked all afternoon toward the peak where the cross stood, passing only gruff men in straw hats tending goats, then, as we neared the top, no one at all. It was your idea that we couldn't look down till we reached the summit.

"No cheating, Simone."

You wanted the vista to hit us in one overwhelming stroke — no dribs and drabs, no gradual seeping in. I scrambled up ahead the last few feet and touched the wooden cross, then turned to look. I felt myself teeter toward the land, which rolled out in all directions, a vast tanned skin of parched mountain and plain declining toward the horizon in minute gradations of brown. The town, with its clay roof tiles, sprawled up the walls of the valley. The sounds were more precise in distance, less cluttered by our own noises: dogs yelped and howled in the endless loop of call and response, while ancient buses groaned up the hills. A woman was calling to her children, her voice spinning effortlessly through the miles of open space. For once I wasn't looking through your eyes, Otto, or even trying to. For once I forgot you were there until suddenly your arms swooped around my waist and tugged me in: this same shirt, I swear, my eyes batting against this hollow of throat.

"I would hardly have recognized you." You reached up and pulled off your cap, regulation New York Yankees model. Your hair, always bushy, had been flattened, and when you ran your hand through it I saw extra streaks of gray.

"Come on, Otto, it hasn't been that long."

"Four or five years."

"Six, actually."

"Really?" You seemed genuinely astonished. "You look fantastic."

I had to smile.

Of course you've got twenty-five years on me — and look it. What's happened to your eyes that used to be so clear and sharply focused? And I have to say this, Otto, your jawline is starting to ripple toward the neck. You seem thinner, more brittle, though I felt the little pot belly when our bodies pressed together. An unexpected squish.

"I look like hell, I know it."

"I wasn't going to say that."

"But you were thinking it, dear."

Dear. That rankled.

We continued to stare at each other, you jiggling change, me stock-still. And I thought, Nothing's happening. The butterflies that had been charging through my stomach all morning seemed to have been drugged. Do you understand what I'm saying, Otto? You stood a foot away and I felt a big fat zero.

"Going to let me in?"

"Of course. Sorry."

You pushed past and I let you poke around the cabin, lifting objects off the mantel: the cracked coil pot, an Indian basket, the black-and-white photo of Father digging the outhouse hole. The woodstove received special attention, and you lifted the burner and peeked inside. I wouldn't have been surprised if you'd reached in and touched the ashes, but you just looked, as if deciding whether I'd chucked something in there to burn. After, you strolled past the coffee table, picked up the book of feminist film criticism, flipped through, and I got the distinct impression you knew it had been selected for display. My cheeks heated up. Your hand swept over the tops of chairs and bookshelves, leaving streaks of shiny wood. Why did I feel you were a scout for some enemy camp, logging facts for a future ambush? I stiffened; the nervous feeling kicked in again. It was almost a relief; this was how I expected to be with you.

I decided to make tea and handed you the kettle so you could fetch water from the outside pump.

"This place is great!" you enthused on your return. "Your dad made it?"

"With my mother."

"It's like ..." You tilted your head. "The house where the seven dwarfs lived. A cartoon cabin." You hunched under the door frame. "Bet your old man is exactly five foot six. Everything's scaled to that height."

Right as always.

I found a box of lemon biscuits and tossed them on the table. You began to make short work of them, knocking two at a time into your hand, while crumbs scattered down the front of your shirt.

"Where's your mother now?" you said, dropping onto a chair.

"She moved into a condo in Etobicoke. Nice view of the lake. She loves it."

"And your dad?"

"He died three and a half years ago."

"I'm so sorry." You winced and briefly shut your eyes. "I didn't know."

"Of course not: how could you?" I pulled away from your reaching hand and watched you swing your legs so you could follow my movements around the room. You didn't speak, and I knew you were hoping I'd say more about him. Your face waited, creased in sympathy. I measured tea into the Brown Betty pot and rinsed out two mugs. I collected the plastic honey jar from the shelf, then poured milk into a tiny pitcher. I would not give you this chance to pry me open. The spoons received a quick wipe on the towel.

You watched each gesture avidly.

"Then will you at least tell me what you've been doing with yourself?"

I let out a breath, staring at the back of my own hand as it closed over the teapot handle. You could still do it, make me achingly visible to myself.

"What do you want to know, Otto?"

"Everything. The works — every second since you left me."

"You think I've been writing it all down, waiting for the day you'd turn up again?"

You smiled quickly. "Haven't you?"

I flushed, because in a way I had. Lived my life and at the same time wondered what you'd make of it, anticipating your comments, your chuckles, and of course, the withering asides that had the effect of turning whatever I was doing — or whoever I was with — into something faintly comical.

"Well?" You leaned forward, following the motion of my fingers as they wrapped around the copper tray. "There must have been plenty of men sniffing around."

You wanted all the details, fixing me with your eyes until I'd find myself describing the color of sheets, the texture

of skin and hair. I set down the tea tray, the smell of Earl Grey
a consoling presence, and pulled up a chair.

"Anyone serious?" you persisted.

"What's all this about, Otto?"

"Curiosity."

"Is that all?"

You hesitated only a second. "Of course."

I stared into your face looking for signs: irony,
amusement ... but could read only the wide-eyed innocence
you'd chosen for display.

I could tell you about Raymond, the dancer — but
stopped just as I saw the edges of your mouth tighten. Already
I was turning Raymond into a story, a series of tiny tropes to
make you howl with delight and commiseration.

I shook my head, half laughing at my narrow escape,
trying to shake that eager stare, at the same time bathing in
its intensity.

"No, Otto, it's my turn."

"Your turn?"

"That's right. My turn to ask questions."

"Ahhh," you exhaled noisily and pushed your chair away
from the table. You lifted your chin toward the window and a
glazed look came over your face that I instantly recognized: the
Shift. The moment of withdrawal. Suddenly, with the practiced
move of an old-time actor, you launched, full-tilt, into a monologue.

Something about light refraction that you'd read in a
scientific journal. "Great diagrams, and a nice sequence of time-
lapse photos ..." Your legs splayed and you crooked an arm over
the back of the chair.

The room shrank.

"... This guy's theory knocks away all our notions of
how we see, how our eyes gather and process light."

I was supposed to lean into every word.

Instead I gazed at you in amazement; you'd known,
hadn't you, exactly what I'd been about to say? The more you
blabbed, underlining every third word with your finger on the
tabletop, the sadder I felt.

And I was bored, Otto.

That was a first.

"... So you just change the angle of dispersal." You hiked a cigarette from the package and positioned it just so on the table. "What appears at first to be pigment is really nothing more than mirrors!" You giggled with delight.

"Otto —"

"Think of what could be done —"

"*Ot-to* —" singing it now like "Yoo-hoo." Nervy. You weren't accustomed to being interrupted in full flight.

Finally you tugged your gaze away from the open window and looked at me.

"I want to know why you're here." I was proud of that, the simple declarative statement.

Our stares hooked for an instant, then, incredibly, you dropped right back into the soliloquy as if I'd never uttered a word.

"... bombard them with photosensitive materials ..."

I saw exactly what was going to happen, how you'd leave with nothing said and that it would drive me crazy and I'd spend the next six months berating myself, reconstructing the scene. So I pushed my chair back and brazenly set my face close to yours.

"Why are you here, Otto? Don't natter on about goddamn light refraction — mail me the article!"

Your cheek muscles worked up and down. Your stare was flat, as if you were overhearing some foreign language. Then you chuckled, flicked an ash off your cigarette, and said, "You haven't yet told me what you've been up to."

You weren't going to be snared by an amateur.

"It's been six years, Otto."

"So work backwards."

Of course. Time is a fluid concept, its direction determined by a tilt of the glass.

"I'm director of the Summer Arts Festival."

A quick smile. "Good for you."

"As of two years ago."

"Still making art?"

"No time." I made a dismissive gesture but felt the familiar pang.

"Of course not. You have a real job. Someone has to run the country."

"It's a big operation," I heard myself insist. "We cram two months full of chamber music, author readings, dance performances, workshops, and classes. Our budget's doubled in two years and most of that is local money." I sounded like the Chamber of Commerce.

You nodded. Smoke drifted from your nostrils and made its languid way toward the ceiling rafters. You were enjoying this. And why not? I was right where I had always been: desperate to please and impress you.

"I'm on a roll," I declared. "They do everything I want. When Krizanc, chairman of my board, starts to rant about 'market-driven programming,' I tell him we have to create our audience. Not let the audience create us. Make them drowsy with something familiar — then kick open the gates. Blow them away!"

Who was this talking?

All these years of careful filtering, reclaiming my voice — and now this: the mimic reborn.

Late-afternoon sun pressed through the window and I leapt to tug the curtain. "It's all in the presentation. Make them think they're on the cutting edge right here in Rupert and it becomes a point of pride. They expect art to be tough; they want it to be."

Your word, as in "tough-minded," "tough-thinking."

"Bravo." You hooked a chair with the toe of your boot. "Sit down, Simone, you're very flushed."

I obeyed, hating the way I felt, overheated and sticky, pulse racing.

"My half-dozen years haven't been nearly so fruitful."

I forced myself to look straight into your face. "What have *you* been doing?"

One of your famous pauses.

"I stayed on," you said at last.

"In San Patricio?"

You nodded.

"What on earth did you do there for six years?" I was shocked; it never occurred to me you might have stayed on. All this time I'd been walking down Spadina Avenue in downtown Toronto every chance I got, glancing up at your studio window, wondering if you were in there with your ripped-up magazines and glue stick.

"Got drunk most days. Made a truckload of bad drawings. Then one morning I got sick of the sun and the smell of rancid cooking oil and started to drive north."

"And?"

"That's it."

"What about your ex —"

"Wife? Carmen's out of the picture, except where Kip is concerned."

Your son. He'd be twenty-one by now. Older than I was when I stepped on the plane to come home. "What's he up to?" You always loved to talk about your son.

Your fingers wrapped around your teacup, the nails chewed to bits. "I saw him this morning. Not so good, Simone. Not so good."

I stared.

"They're adjusting his medication. Makes him screwy, his equilibrium is shot. The kid can hardly walk."

"Medication? What are you talking about?" My self-consciousness vanished.

"He gets seizures." Your eyes scanned the room without focusing. "It began five or six years ago. Of course, you'd have no way of knowing."

"What kind of seizures?"

"He goes months without any problem, then suddenly keels over wherever he is: the gym, a crowded subway."

"Jesus, Otto, I had no idea."

"Of course not."

"It doesn't have anything to do with" — I struggled to sound casual — "that time he fell off the boat?"

"What?"

You sounded genuinely mystified.

"In San Patricio, on the lake." I prodded, already wishing I hadn't brought it up.

You stared at me, fully engaged for a few seconds. "I don't see how. He wasn't under more than a minute."

Right.

"The worst of it isn't the seizures," you went on. "Which happen maybe three, four times a year. It's his attitude that stinks. Yesterday, at the hospital, he made his neck go all floppy, then titters, 'What a shame your kid's a crip.' Crip my ass!"

The table shuddered as you smacked it with your hand. "Ninety-five percent of the time he's perfectly okay. There's guys a lot worse off than him — blind! Imagine being blind, or deaf! But you don't see them hanging out on Queen Street, playing skinhead, cadging cigarettes and spare change. He snorts PAM out of a goddamn baggie ..." You took a deep breath and snapped open the top of your shirt. "He's quit three schools, got caught boosting a pair of Doc Martens from the Eaton Centre ..."

Had you driven two hours to spout off against your son, ask my forgiveness for being such a lousy father?

"I'm sorry, Otto."

"So am I." Your tone was aggressive, as if you were determined I'd know the worst of it. "I thought if I stayed far away in some hill town everyone would be better off, that I was so fucked up it would overwhelm them. Pure ego." You laughed. "Which I've never been short of."

I didn't deny this. "He lives with you, or Carmen?"

"He's in a halfway house for kids who screw up. They huddle out on the sidewalk most of the day, smoking, or they're taking courses in something called 'Life Skills.' " You snorted. "He asked after you, just as I was leaving today."

"Me?" My mind was racing.

"He wondered if you were 'still on the scene.' "

"What did you say?"

"That I hadn't seen you for years. That it wasn't meant to be." Your knee pressed against mine. "He's convinced you saved his life, that time he pitched overboard."

I reddened. "That's absurd."

"Even so, he likes the idea that you pulled him from the brink."

"But it's not true!"

"He thinks it is."

First your knee, now your thigh. Uneasy, I shifted, but didn't move away.

You reached for the cookie box and shook it. Empty.

This wasn't the scene I'd been picturing, far from it.

Hell, I was feeling sorry for you. I'd been prepared for anger — even desire, but not this.

"Sometimes I used to feel you two were conspiring against me." You spoke with studied casualness. "When you came in from riding those underfed nags, Kip was so flushed and healthy-looking — I used to wish I had that power."

Power? I had to laugh. So you were jealous, Otto. This notion would have pleased me once. Now I just felt drained. The numbness crept back. Here we were again, using Kip as our topic, and I was supposed to pretend I cared. I reached for the tea things and scraped cookie crumbs onto a saucer.

A long time ago I was reaching for you to tear the world open. Now, in your presence, I felt hemmed in, claustrophobic.

"I need to live in Toronto again, to be near Kip."

"That makes sense." I didn't hide a yawn.

"Last Saturday I picked up the newspaper and who did I see but you — with this most professional smile planted on your face. Very impressive, Simone."

"You saw that?" I couldn't help feeling pleased. The *Globe* had done a feature in the Arts section, underlining how the Summer Festival had "revitalized" the area and pinning much of the success on its "fresh, young director."

"I thought, She looks so damn competent — pretty too."

I crumpled the cookie box and tossed it toward the trash.

"I'm flat broke, Simone. Benny says the art market's shriveled, nothing's moving, nothing he can do for me."

Benny — your dealer.

"There's a recession, Otto. Even in San Patricio you must have heard about it."

"I need a job."

"Right." I still didn't get it.

"So —" You followed me to the sink with your saucer and cup. "You're running this nice little festival. You could fit me in, as a teacher, artist-in-residence. I'm flexible as an old shoe, and more to the point, I'm desperate." A smoke ring escaped from your mouth and hung in the air.

"As a teacher," you continued, "I'm the best there is. You, if anyone, should know that."

I dumped the leaves into the compost bowl. Now I understood why you'd come.

"We always got along well."

I stared, mouth open.

You were jiggling a set of keys: Budget Rent A Car. At least I was right about that. "Think about it. Drop me a line, or call, soon as you get a moment. I've got my old studio back."

The little Honda bucked down the hill until its muffler scraped highway asphalt.

Then you cranked your window down and shouted into the hot still air: "You must feel very safe here!"

I opened my mouth to protest — "Who the hell wants safety?" — then remembered: they were your exact words, uttered years earlier.

It was a scruffy copy of *Lassie Come Home*, borrowed from the Rupert Public Library, and as I turned each page my fingers buffed scabs of peanut butter and petrified snot.

I didn't even notice the sun was falling and I was losing my light. I simply tilted the book a little more every few minutes — until a word stopped my eye mid-sentence.

What was this word?

She.

Lassie, I'd just discovered, was a "she."

The book dropped between my knees. Lassie, the hero of the tale, was actually a heroine. That was like those other despised words; poetess, actress, cowgirl — images of women in fringed skirts, riding sidesaddle, squealing with terror. How could I identify with the girl version of the real thing? How can fantasy be populated by underachievers?

2

"WHAT IS THIS?" You picked a length of rope out of your knapsack and swept it across the desk.

No one spoke.

"What is this?" you repeated, drawing the rope under the table, wrapping it around one of the legs, then tugging it free.

There was a sound like the cracking of a whip.

"No ideas?"

The rope skittered along the paint-flecked floor, then suddenly you were dragging it up your body, bending every which way.

"It's a piece of rope," someone said at last. A man of about thirty and he sounded wary, like he was afraid you were making fun of us.

You continued to slither the rope up your leg, across your belly and chest, and around your neck.

"A snake," someone offered.

You paid absolutely no attention to these lame-brain answers. The rope cut through your hair, then suddenly you leapt up onto the desk, swung your legs over, and lay down.

The rope circled your neck, looped down your side then between your legs, never stopping its journey. A cigarette dangled out the side of your mouth, chucking ash onto the floor. This despite a prominently placed NO SMOKING sign. People were starting to laugh nervously. Behind your prone form was the door and stuck to it a second sign: DRAWING: EXPERIMENTAL TECHNIQUES.

"A line!" I burst out. "It's a line!"

Your hand stopped moving. You lifted your head off the desk and stared at us.

"Who said that?"

Your voice was brusque, almost accusing.

"I did." Straddling my workbench, half hidden by a drawing board, I managed to wave. At nineteen I was the youngest in the class.

"What's your name?"

"Simone Paris."

"Well, Simone Paris, you're right."

Everyone was looking at me.

You swung your legs over the edge of the desk and slipped off. Your eyes, which were puffy as if you never got enough sleep, took in the whole class — a dozen of us sitting in a loose semi-circle, still obediently watchful.

"If I were one of those swamis," you said, "I'd swallow this entire length of rope and haul it up for you, right from my guts. Because a line must be as unprincipled and vulgar as possible. A line —" pause — "is rude. Not graceful or delicate — but rude." You grabbed the rope, stuck it under your armpit, and drew it out slowly. "Never shy." You strung it under your groin then hitched it out the other side. To do this you had to bend way over so we were staring at the curve of your spine.

More nervous giggles. But not from me. I was riveted by your performance. I'd never seen anything like it.

"A line has no brain." You had straightened up. "Of course, you think you do. Like any civilized person, you cultivate grace and restraint. You dislike, above all ..." You hesitated, giving us plenty of time to fill in the word. You lit a fresh cigarette, cupped the match in your hand, and blew it out.

"Bad smells!"

No one laughed, but you did. A great booming delighted laugh.

"Who does he think he is?" the whispers started.

I sat as tall as I could on the bench, backbone rigid, eyes fixed ahead. If I forgot to blink for an hour it was because I was afraid I'd miss something. You wore patched jeans, a red shirt with pearl buttons, and a frayed denim jacket. It wasn't your face I stared at, but your body. You moved in slow, thought-out gestures that worked to look relaxed, but I could see you were wound up so tight the whole performance threatened to crumble.

"Chances are ..." You leaned against the desk with one knee bent. An endless pause. Had you forgotten what you were going to say? When you tilted the sole of your cowboy boot I saw it had been mended with a strip of green linoleum.

"Chances are you already know how to draw well enough. I'm here to teach you how to think." You scanned the guarded faces of our little group. "I won't bother looking at your portfolios because, frankly, I'm not the least interested in what you've done before you entered this room."

You paused to let this sink in. You paid absolutely no attention to the chorus of grumblings and muttered comments. If anything, you seemed to enjoy the effect of your declarations, the growing hostility on the faces of normally good-natured townspeople.

"Let's get down to it," someone said.

"I came here to draw, not listen to this kook."

"You." Your finger aimed at a middle-aged woman in a smock. I'd seen her behind the counter at the craft store in Rupert. She always wore heavy handmade jewelry and batik headbands. "I'd like you to sit on this chair where we can get a good look at you."

"Am I to be the model?"

"Don't worry, madam, you may keep your clothes on."

"I intend to, Mr. Guest."

She sat down on the chair, crossing her legs and arms, and stared up at you, unintimidated.

"Good. Now." You glanced at the rest of us. "Put your pencils down. Sit on your hands. This is an exercise in concentration. You are training your minds." You tapped your skull with an index finger. "Remember, eyes are not only the way in, but the way out. In and out. Seepage and drainage; the perfect ecological system."

"For Pete's sake," someone said. "What's he talking about?"

"Shhh," I hissed angrily. This was important, this was new. My brain clenched, ready for anything.

"You will draw this woman." You glanced at her. "What's your name?"

"Samantha Rice-Keeley."

"You will draw Samantha in great detail but you will make no mark on the paper. You will use your eyes and brain only. You will trace every part of her, not just edges, not just skin, not just features. Allow your imagined line to explore every inch of her person."

Samantha Rice-Keeley squirmed a little, then tossed her head back.

"If for some reason your mind begins to wander and you lose track of the line — start again. The beginning is here." You touched the small of her back. "As for you —" Your hand trailed up her spine. "Imagine all those lines creeping over your body."

For a second Samantha Rice-Keeley shut her eyes.

The room went perfectly quiet, except for the buzz of the overhead fluorescent bulbs.

I set my hands on my knees, leaned forward, and imagined a thick black line uncoiling, almost rubbery in texture, as it moved over the curves of Samantha Rice-Keeley's plump form.

Twice I lost it and had to jump back to the beginning. It was like landing on the big 88 in Snakes and Ladders. The first time was because I glanced up; I wanted to see if you were watching me. You weren't. In fact, your eyes were shut and you sat cross-legged on the desk breathing deeply.

The second time came just before the end of the exercise. I was intent on the journey over fleshy mountain and plain, leaving an imaginary inky trail behind. My eyes grew wider as I fought off the need to blink. Was I drawing a real pencil over paper? Did it matter? I was dizzy with concentration.

"Breathe!"

I let out a surprised gasp. You were standing at my side.

"Don't forget to breathe, dear. You'll keel over."

"What on earth do you need to take a course for? Just draw. That's the only way to learn. There's no short cut." Father launched into the speech I'd heard him deliver a dozen times to representatives of the Ministry of Education. "To understand anything we must experience it directly. This can only be accomplished by doing, by finding our own way. A teacher is the most intrusive being on earth. To think we give them our young minds to muck about in!"

It had been a struggle to get into this classroom.

"You're already an artist," he pointed out.

The cabin was full of my work, starting from the stick figures of a three-year-old to my current Daliesque eyeballs peering through intense cloud cover.

"I want to learn more," I said firmly. "I want to meet other people."

"She has a point," Mother said, and she looked for an instant toward the window where night reflected back an image of herself in the big upholstered chair.

At the end of the first class you gave us an exercise to do at home.

"This time," you said graciously, "you may make marks on paper. Take an object of moderate size —" You paused, waiting for suggestions.

"A vase of flowers," someone said.

"A musical instrument."

"A banana."

I searched my mind for some object bizarre enough to impress you. A clump of dirt? Rubber boot? I thought you looked at me, waiting, but I just shook my head, furious at losing the opportunity.

"Place this object you've chosen on a neutral surface, then make a hundred drawings."

"A hundred?" someone squeaked.

"Each will be slightly different, for after each attempt you will twist this object slightly — and draw it again."

"I don't have time," a pudgy woman in a tank top complained.

I turned around and glared at her.

"I got six kids to chase around after. I came here to rest."

Rest! Stupid woman. Art is not a holiday! I was indignant on your behalf and waited for you to venture some withering comment. It didn't come. Instead you spoke in a quiet, almost tender voice.

"I don't want to add to your duties. If you can only work in class, that's fine."

I felt a pang of dismay, noting the way you looked at this woman, who seemed to me well over the hill. Your face softened, the nervous edge disappeared; for that instant you were human-size and she'd somehow caused it.

As everyone packed up I scoured my mind for some way to approach you; a question, a clever comment or observation. You had to realize I wasn't an ordinary student; I was here to learn everything you had to offer. A hundred drawings? Hell, I'd do a thousand. While the others left, bewildered and grumbling, I hung back, repacking my little sack of Conté pencils and crayons. I carefully rolled up the sheets of blank paper and slipped an elastic over them. We hadn't made a mark all evening. My heart was racing as I watched you drop your own things into a worn leather knapsack. I could see why you weren't interested in the portfolios of my fellow students — meticulous drawings of barns and gnarled driftwood. I'd seen some of these earlier and, I confess, had been overwhelmed by their accomplishment. But I was onto something different. I had penetrated the surfaces of people and objects and revealed their true natures. I mentally flipped through my work: the landscape that looks utterly normal until you notice the small, angry eye hanging between the upper branches of a pine. And I had another one with this half-human, half-wolf creature bleeding on the snow.

I could modestly let the ribbon fall loose: first prize, watercolor, Annual Huron County Juried Youth Exhibition.

You ran a hand through your hair and glanced at me. There was something about your cheekbones that was almost Indian. Later you'd tell me a grandmother was part Mohawk. What about my image of the skyscraper melting into the barren post-nuclear landscape? Mother said it gave her the creeps; she could hardly bear to look at it. I called it "Toxic Landscape," and it had even got written up in the local newspaper. They called it a "harrowing post-apocalyptic vision."

"Will you turn the lights off, dear?"

You were speaking to me. I darted a look over my shoulder; we were the only ones left in the room. Now or never. I smiled and said with brusque confidence, "I wonder if you'd just take a look at these," and slid my portfolio across the desk.

You stared at it.

I felt my toes grip the inside of my shoes.

You glanced at the clock, sighed, then without lowering your pack, lifted the edge of the portfolio and flipped it over.

"Toxic Landscape" was on top. You barely glanced at it. Instead you picked up the sheaf of paintings and drawings and let them drop one by one, like someone sifting through for a lost bill.

My hands fastened to the sides of my body. What exactly was I expecting? Only that you would exclaim with astonishment, "Where did you learn to do this?"

I waited.

There was a look on your face, amused perhaps, and completely unsurprised.

"The hairy-eyeball-apocalyptic school," you said, letting the portfolio drop shut.

You were already reaching for the panel of lights while a silent scream of humiliation tore through my body.

They watched as I roamed the front room of the cabin, seizing things then dropping them one by one; first the off-kilter vase Mother had made during her clay period, then father's attempt at a rainwater siphon, which leaked so badly it could never be used ... Didn't they see themselves? The place was make-believe, some kind of stage set. A cartoon cabin.

"Just what I was afraid of." Father refolded his *Guardian* and prodded the crossword puzzle with a fingertip wound in dental floss. "She'll be joining the Moonies next. Look at her."

I was hunched over the dining table, executing drawing number sixty-two of a ball. That red Swedish ball Mother used in one of her exercise routines.

"I say sign her out while we can still get our deposit back."

But we all knew it was too late.

"A line is rude," I chanted to myself. My hand, which had been cramped for years, began to stride boldly over the page.

"What's the point of all this?" Father sifted through the pile of almost identical drawings. There was a perplexed look on his face, and his glasses, mended with Band-Aids and bits of wire, were pushed to the end of his nose.

I glanced up and said witheringly, "Eyes are not only the way in, but the way out."

"It's certainly possible to learn to swim without feeling you have to cross the English Channel." He clasped his hands in front of his stomach and flexed them until his fingers gave a satisfying crack. He wore navy blue trunks.

I had no choice but to follow. I was nine years old and I knew he wouldn't give up. The usual sense of doom clung as I slid down the path to the narrow strip of beach. Huge limestone boulders looked ready to lunge forward and topple into the water.

"I'm over here."

As if I didn't know. Father, all five foot six inches of him, stood waist deep.

"Come on," he waved.

I peeled off my shirt and shorts and instantly felt my skin pebble in the breeze. I stepped cautiously into the water and tried to smile bravely. There was always the chance he'd take pity on me.

"At your age I was like a dolphin, every chance I could I'd swim — and that was in Saskatoon, on the prairie!"

I knew this story — how he'd found any scrap of water to paddle around in: a swollen creek, a reservoir at night, a rich person's pool ...

I stared at the water trying to see where the sand ended so I wouldn't stub my toe.

"For Pete's sake, Simone, it's not even up to your belly button."

His favorite days were right after a storm when the sky was a hard blue and the lake, as if belonging to another landscape, churned a muddy gray, each wave frilled as it crashed onto the beach. He'd zigzag across our little bay, trolling through the water with his steady stroke, head lifting to one side, then the other, seeking air.

"Fall into the water. Let it carry you. Don't fight it!" he commanded.

"You mean drown!"

He snapped the waist of his trunks again and sighed. "Grab onto my shoulders."

He actually thought this was fun. He didn't know how terrifying it was to cling onto someone who wasn't touching ground. His back was hairy and slippery. When he dove into a huge breaker, did he really expect me to follow? Instead I let go and felt the water sweep me to where there was no up or down, and no sound but the wave's own roar. It felt like forever, lungs pressing against my backbone before the wave pitched me ashore like a clump of soggy seaweed. I lay there, belly cleaving a ditch in the sand. He didn't see me at first. I had plenty of time to watch him frantically scan the waves.

"Simone! Where the blazes did you go?"

I waited longer than necessary before lifting a frail hand.

"Over here."

His face was white, his chest sucked in.

As he helped me back up the cliff he said in a quiet voice, "We needn't tell your mother about this."

He was shivering so hard I couldn't stand the touch of him. When I was under there, inside the lake, what use had he been?

☀ *3* ☀

NOBODY MADE A hundred drawings, except me. Most did a dozen or so careful renderings on acid-free paper. We took turns displaying our efforts across the long desk in front of the room. Despite previous skepticism, each student looked to you and only you for criticism and admiration. For the longest time you said not a word, bending over, looking carefully or carelessly (we were never certain) at each offering. One hopeful had sketched a glove, another an artfully arranged wad of paper, another a trowel. I was completely intimidated by my classmates' drawings; they seemed marvelous and professional, the perspective perfectly achieved. What did I think I was up to with my stubby marker? Suddenly I longed for the confidence of my old way of working, back when being an artist seemed completely possible. Samantha Rice-Keeley displayed three — only three — drawings of a child's clown doll. Each, I thought, was charged with energy, the line vigorous, filling immense sheets of paper. She knew it too. Her hands dug deep into the pockets of her paint-spattered smock.

She wore heavy lipstick, the color of the raspberries that were in season. Silver earrings jingled as she tossed her hair. We awaited your verdict.

"Uh-huh," you said, and tapped your knuckles on the desk. Then suddenly you picked up one of her sketches and began to rip it. There was a collective gasp of horror. You continued to tear — not randomly, but with the intent of liberating a distinct section of the drawing.

"This —" you lifted a pie-shaped wedge whose content was an unrecognizable crisscross of line and shade — "is a nice drawing."

Samantha Rice-Keeley's mouth dropped a mile.

When my turn came I was ready to fly out of the room. I thought I'd been so clever choosing a subject that looked identical no matter which way it was turned. Mother's Swedish ball was now represented by a stack of a hundred sheets of newsprint on the desk.

Everyone laughed. It was funny. I mean, who on earth would go to such extremes?

You didn't laugh. Instead, you picked up the drawings one by one, all hundred of them, giving each effort a dozen seconds of your attention.

We stood silently, compelled to respect this ritual by some sense of decorum, sipping our coffee and shifting weight. The wall clock clicked and the big hand shot forward. Finally, and it must have taken twenty minutes, you reached the final drawing. It looked almost exactly like the others, only by this time my hand had become cramped and I'd skimped on the shading. You looked at this one more intently, then collected all the papers, shook them so their edges were aligned, and passed them back to me.

"Yes," you said. "Yes."

Yes. The word swam in front of my eyes, all waving fins and glittering scales.

Only I had understood the true nature of the exercise. My attempt, though technically clumsy, was more poetic than the others.

Did you have any idea what you'd set in motion? All your gestures and words were so choreographed, so calculated in effect — but you couldn't have been prepared for me.

At break Artie passed around his copy of *C* magazine, folded back to a photograph of you posing in front of a massive green painting. I waited my turn impatiently, then seized the magazine. I couldn't read the piece fast enough, skimming through the dense critical language — "for this double gesture, reductionism and production of the sublime ..." — to get to the personal bits.

"Guest considers himself a totally urban painter, tied to the clamor of city streets."

There was a caption under the photo, pegged in quotations: "When I look at a painting I want to laugh at the absence of illusion."

The phrase entered my brain surgically: I understood exactly what you meant, the way an astronaut lifting into space suddenly comprehends the meaning of infinity.

My eyes strayed back to the photograph: you standing in front of the painting, arms folded, wearing acrylic-encrusted chinos, a black T-shirt, and an amused expression, as if you knew exactly how all this would look.

The issue was being torn from my hands.

"Let me see that, dear."

I recognized the sequined voice of Samantha Rice-Keeley.

You had another exercise for us, this time to be executed in class.

"We will choose partners and take turns being model and — artisan."

I got the idea you couldn't bear to use the word "artist" anywhere near us.

"You will sit facing one another and remain very quiet. No yapping. The artisan will shut his eyes and perform the drawing using only his sense of touch as guide."

"Oh boy," someone moaned. "Encounter-group time."

"No," you said sharply. "This has nothing to do with emotions or squeamishness or psychology. This is to do with paying attention."

You set up two of us as a demonstration: a thirtyish man with tufty sideburns, and a woman who was over seventy and always wore gardening overalls to class.

"Close your eyes, Joe. You right-or left-handed?"

"Right."

"Then use that hand to touch Miss Dykstra's face. Very slowly mark the contours of her features, trace the textures of her skin — and never lift your fingers. Your left hand will draw what you feel. And only what you feel. Banish memory of what she looks like, what any face looks like. Draw what the tips of your fingers tell you."

We paired up. I made a quick count. There were nine students tonight (three had dropped out after the first class): an uneven number. I buried my face in my satchel as if searching for something, meeting no one's eye. Harry, a man my father's age who ran the Chrysler franchise, started across the floor toward me but when I twisted my face away he quickly swerved off.

Good.

There was only me left — and you. I looked about the room in feigned dismay. "What will I do?"

You came to the rescue.

"I'll be your model."

"Since there's no one else ..." I shrugged.

Were you fooled for a minute?

Your forehead felt slightly coarse and pebbly, like the limestone that jutted into the bay, which I loved to stroke, imagining I could wear it smooth. My fingers took shy sweeps back and forth and I felt something tighten, just the faintest shifting beneath. Were you frowning? I wasn't allowed to peek. My eyes stayed glued shut. I didn't think at all about my left hand, which scribbled away; every ounce of my attention went to that section of heat where my skin met yours. At first I was afraid to move anywhere near your eyes: what if I poked them by mistake? Yet after a few experimental swerves I fluttered across your eyebrows, then onto your lids, and immediately felt them fold shut. I lingered there, where the skin is so thin and soft, feeling the pulse and flicker of your eyeballs beneath. I thought of newborn birds, their membranes thin and transparent. After, I found the cavities around the base of your nose and shimmied up onto the bridge, which was sharp and bony. This Braille encounter was a miniature landscape where the rest of the world receded. I lost all sense of time; the classroom disappeared, in fact you disappeared. You had become a journey of texture and form; the delicacy of eyelids, the prickliness of cheeks that hadn't been shaved since morning. It was my first lesson in abstraction.

When I was through I opened my eyes and squinted into the mauve haze of fluorescent light. You were staring at me. Your upper lip moved as if you meant to say something. Instead you took a very long breath, held it, and sighed deeply.

("Otto?" I asked a couple of months later. We were sitting in the front seat of your camper looking down at the lake, which was a churlish gray. "That time I touched your face during the blind exercise —"

"Don't remind me," you groaned, leaning your chest into the steering wheel. "I had such a hard-on."

"You did?" I was thrilled. Then I had a sudden image; your hands cradled on your lap, flexing to make a sort of table, or shield.)

The next class I was eager to see how you would greet me. I would pass slowly by your desk and trail my left hand over its surface: a subtle hinge to memory.

I did this.

You glanced up and three lines creased between your eyes, making a fan of disapproval. After the briefest hesitation, you continued unpacking; a magazine, a clump of pencils, postcards.

Scorched, I crossed the floor to my bench. For the first time I was relieved when my classmates shuffled in, chatting, so easy in their greetings.

"Saw you swimming by the pier this morning, Otto."

They had nothing at stake; they inhabited a different universe.

I hadn't even got around to calling you "Otto" to your face.

It didn't get better.

The next three classes you studiously ignored me. It was as if I'd offended you in some way. When I asked a question, you stared right over my head, and answered with barely concealed irritation. Looking at my work, you would simply nod and mumble something before moving on to the next student. Once I saw you giggling with Samantha Rice-Keeley, reaching out and touching her earring, which was in the shape of a hand.

"You made this?"

"My daughter did."

"I bet she's something."

Suddenly there were only two classes left. Then you would return to Toronto, to your life.

(Later you said, by way of explanation, not apology, "I could feel your need, Simone. It blinked like neon and frankly I couldn't deal with it; my own life was such a mess.")

The second-to-last Wednesday evening I was ready to give up. To hell with you. I'd done my exercise, a collage using rolls of the dice to determine the position of images on a grid. I expected nothing. I didn't even try to catch your eye, and instead of elbowing to the front with my work I hung back, propping myself against the wall. Seeing this, you relented.

"Nice effort, Simone. You didn't cheat."

Others had, re-situating the torn bits of magazine paper to create a more pleasing image.

"The idea here," you went on, "is to get around habits of arrangement, subvert our own banal tastes." You didn't stop looking at me.

I glanced down at my feet, smiling.

I knew that.

At coffee break we congregated around the open window, flexing cramped hands, sipping vending-machine coffee, listening to Joe describe how he was going to build himself a studio over the garage and start a print shop. You kept peeling the lid off your coffee cup and replacing it, and munching trail mix out of a zip-lock bag. You stood slightly apart from the rest of us, just enough to make the point without being unsociable. Sometimes you disappeared completely during break, and once I'd spied you striding across the parking lot, head bent, smoking furiously.

"I'll hitch a skylight onto the dormer and let the sun pour through!" Joe declared, pushing his hands into his pockets, waiting for comments.

Tossing back a third of your coffee, you rubbed your mouth hard and spoke.

"I always thought I'd been a good husband, a good father. Perhaps not the best provider in the world — but two out of three ain't bad. And now she tells me" — you finished off the coffee, wincing at either its foul taste or something else — "that she doesn't want me around any more."

There was an awful silence.

They looked down at the floor, out the window, into their coffee. I stared into your face.

They were afraid to hear more: I didn't know enough to be afraid.

Your face held an expression of complete bewilderment. You crumpled your cup and sent it sailing toward the wastebasket.

"Bull's-eye!" you cried.

The next session was our last. You'd arranged an outing, a field trip to the studio of a well-known local sculptor, Charles Townley. Townley had several pieces, you informed us, in the National Gallery in Ottawa. More impressive was the fact he was represented by some hot-shot New York dealer.

"Megabucks." You rubbed your hands.

We met at the school and formed a car pool. You'd gone ahead so I ended up in Samantha Rice-Keeley's car, squished in the back seat between Joe and Artie.

Charles Townley's "barn" was a spectacular three-story studio high on the ridge overlooking both the valley and the bay. It was invisible from the highway. Artie counted hydro poles leading up the long private drive.

"Twelve. Jesus, figure what that cost!"

You were already there when we arrived. Townley, a hefty man of perhaps forty, with a full beard and dressed in baggy coveralls, was laughing, evidently at something you'd said. Beside him you seemed thin and sharp-featured, rolling on the balls of your feet, pushing your face a fraction too close to his.

We tumbled out of the cars and introduced ourselves. Townley clasped our hands and bellowed to each in turn, "Welcome to the workshop. Take a look around."

Massive steel constructions were placed among the trees like the leavings of some high-tech army. Their surfaces ranged from the deep red of corroded Cor-Ten steel to a freshly foundried gunmetal gray.

"They all move." Townley encouraged us to get up close and investigate. One piece you sat on and a long beam would swing you slowly back and forth while your feet grazed the grass. Another you climbed up on, fitting hands and feet into little grooves — until the thing suddenly shifted and you found yourself scooped into the air.

"Hey!" I yelped, holding on for dear life.

"Hang on tight, dear!" Townley shouted back. "Enjoy the view."

Afterwards he said, "Can't show that one in public. The insurance boys take one look and howl."

We were rounded up and directed inside the barn.

It was impressive. There were huge radial-arm saws and band saws, drill presses and lathes. I spotted a blasting furnace and welding gear, then crooked my neck to stare at the ductwork and massive ceiling beams. A catwalk held storage areas containing sheets of steel, piles of lumber, all sorts of found objects: hubcaps, rubber tires, furniture odds and ends, the rusted hull of a motorboat, all neatly sorted.

Townley good-naturedly gave us a tour, waving off our little cries of astonishment with corny jokes. Pointing at the rusted boat he remarked, "The wife sends me to sleep here when I've had a few."

A bathtub, a diseased-looking object with corroded sides and unpleasant stains, was straddling a forklift.

"Haven't decided where this baby's going to go. But don't old tubs make you feel sentimental?" He ran his huge hand over the side where the porcelain was still intact.

I heard someone snort and twisted around to see. You were smiling innocently.

After the tour we found things to sit on: toolboxes, crates, a worktable. A telephone rang half a dozen times before the answering machine clicked in. Next to it a fax started rattling.

Glancing at these machines, Townley made a face. "The fucking world; it never leaves you alone."

There was a second snort, and this time I didn't need to spin round to know where it came from.

We were to ask questions and he would attempt to answer them.

"Anything you want, don't be shy."

Townley affected a folksy chumminess. His responses took the form of stories or anecdotes and were never even faintly intellectual. He sprawled on a decaying leather chair like some deposed king and drank whiskey out of a jelly jar.

While he spoke you wandered around examining not the art, but the tools: the huge saws and planes and sanders. At one point Townley paused in his description of "raw tonnage" and said, "Don't smoke in here, man, this place is a firetrap."

You pulled the butt from your mouth and carefully ground it on the sole of your boot. I glimpsed your face: lips tugged taut.

"I admire this guy." Townley waved a muscular arm toward you. "I've been looking at his work for fifteen years and he's stuck to his guns. Otto's a true-blue modernist, none of the post-this neo-that bullshit. Right, Guest?"

You took your time answering. First, you wiped your mouth with the back of your hand, then you chuckled in an affected way.

"You don't have a goddamn clue what I'm up to, Townley."

You knocked a fresh cigarette out of your pack, lit it, then pulled it out of your mouth, miming astonishment.

"Nothing went 'Boom!'" You scanned the room, fixing each of us in your stare. "So much for danger, and risk."

Townley watched this performance with strained good humor and hoisted the jelly jar to his lips.

"Want to know what it costs to build one of those big suckers out there? How do I haul up —"

"I've got a question." You pushed forward until you were half a dozen feet from our host. "Tell me, Townley, are you projecting images, cranking from the natural world onto the body's field, or the reverse?"

Charles Townley made a clicking sound with his mouth. "I don't think like that, man."

Unfazed, you continued. "Do you see yourself as working in a quasi-scientific mode?"

You didn't seem to get it. Instead of backing off you kept going, asking a convoluted question no one could make sense of, dragging in terms like "auto-referential" and "contextual tissue." Townley's face clouded over and he pushed aside his coverall, revealing an ample belly clad in a Jim Beam T-shirt. He began to ostentatiously scratch himself.

There was nervous tittering while you droned on.
"... to the mistake of materiality?" The question finally
ground to a halt.

There was a tense silence, which Townley broke by
saying, "Hell, is that all? You were just getting into a groove.
Why quit now, Guest? I bet these folks would pay a dollar just
to hear you have another crack at it."

Without thinking, I cleared my throat and pushed out
a question of my own. Some drivel about the "kinetic impulse"
as a driving force in his work.

Harry, who was perched on an upended bucket,
raised his eyebrows.

Townley studied me for a few seconds, then said,
"What else is there but the fucking kinetic impulse?" He leapt
from his chair and was suddenly crouching by my side,
rubbing a furry cheek against mine. "Two surfaces collide," he
stage-whispered. "That's where the heat is."

My classmates snickered.

I didn't. It seemed natural that he should pick me out,
see that I wasn't like the others.

His eyes were brown, his breath a rich mix of whiskey
and tobacco.

"Whoa!" Townley rubbed his cheek, then mine, with
his fingertips. "This one's on fire!"

He was looking straight at you, as if waiting for some
sign, but you just glared back. Finally, he heaved himself to his
feet, pressing into my shoulder for support.

"That's all, folks. I got a commission due for a baby
Rockefeller end of the week."

As we clumped through high grass to the cars I saw a vintage
Harley-Davidson propped against a stone wall. For a moment
I wondered if it was real, or another sculpture.

"Drive back with me." A hand pressed against my spine.

I didn't have to look.

"Sure," I nodded, not missing a beat.

As we approached the truck your hand swept down my back and rested, just for an instant — but long enough to know what it was doing — on my behind.

"You decided to save me from myself back there. Why?"

Keeping my eyes straight ahead, I smiled. My skin tingled in a line straight up my spine to the top of my head. I didn't answer.

"The guy wanted to deck me — who could blame him."

We pushed through the tall grass, batting at tiny gnats and sleepy wasps sprayed by sunlight. We passed fifty feet from Townley's home, a modest brick farmhouse with the original wooden porch straddling two sides. Sheets and towels and massive T-shirts, each with a different logo, flapped from a line at the back. I could smell soap as a breeze tossed through the stiffened cotton.

"Meet Molly." You drove one of those Toyota pickups converted into a camper. The bumper was held on with rope and I had to tug hard at the passenger door before it swung open. Once inside, I fit my feet around a stack of yellowed newspapers, lifted a loose-leaf notebook from the seat and found a place for it on the floor, then moved quickly to rescue a pile of cassettes that had begun to slide off the dashboard onto my lap. I cranked open the window with one hand and searched, without success, for a seatbelt with the other.

"The man's an idiot!" You hit the wheel with your fist and I realized your breath was working in short rasps, as if you'd been running. "He's decided the intellect is too scary to consider. He's made a fucking fortune building those overgrown toys."

I was still too happy to take your anger seriously. "What's wrong with that?"

You stared. "Haven't you learned anything from me, Simone?"

Chastened, I didn't answer. Had I really been taken in by the oversize studio, the good-old-boy presence of Charles

Townley? You'd immediately seen through all that: the man
was a fool. An anti-intellectual numskull.

I remembered the heat of your hand as it shimmied
down my backbone.

"'Two surfaces collide,'" you snorted and simultaneously
fired the ignition. "Did you like having that hairy cheek scrape
yours?"

"Not especially," I lied.

We backed into Townley's raspberry bushes before
shooting down the hill.

"Where can I drop you?"

I understood you had to ask this question.

"My bike is back at the school."

We drove on a while in silence.

"How old are you, Simone?"

"Nineteen. Twenty in November."

You nodded, considering this. "I'm forty-five, forty-
six in May — if I live that long." This was followed by a
dry laugh.

We were passing the Hogarth Ranch, a huge spread
with two training rings and a dozen purebred horses, half of
them kin to Northern Dancer.

"Nineteen." You shook your head. "That's awfully young."

"Not to me; it's older than anything I've been so far."

You thought this was funny and giggled on and off for
the next mile. We passed Colony Bay Antiques and Collectibles
with its sprawling lawn littered with rusting farm equipment,
and suddenly your arm slid over the back of the seat and I felt
your fingers brush my neck.

"I like you, Simone."

I didn't move.

"I got a fifteen-year-old son at home."

I didn't see what this had to do with anything.

"Carmen — my wife," you continued, "has turfed me
out of the house. She's discovered she doesn't need me." Your

voice was level, uninflected. "She's taken up with the kid who installs the shows."

"Shows?"

For some reason my mind shot to trapezes and lion tamers.

"My wife is Carmen Deems-Guest."

I got the idea I was supposed to be impressed.

"Oh?"

"That means nothing to you?" Your hand drifted over my neck to my shoulder.

"Not really."

Fingers tucked under my shirt and grazed my collarbone. "She's the hottest dealer in the country. Most young artists spring to attention at the sound of her name."

"I guess I — "

"Don't apologize." We were slowing down, in the middle of nowhere. "Do you have to go home now?"

"No."

"Would you like to see some of my work?"

The summer school had put you up at Bo-Peep Cabins, twenty-five acres of campsites and a dozen tiny cabins with pitched roofs. You were number 12, planted under the shade of a huge uncropped spruce. On the door was a gouged-wood Bo-Peep figure on tiptoes peeking through the window.

"She's always there." You pretended to lift the edge of her stiff skirt. "Rain or shine."

I'd skimmed over the grass in a kind of dream; it was going to happen. Whatever "it" was.

The door unlocked, you heaved your knapsack and a carton of cigarettes onto the floor. The interior of the cabin was austere: one small room, a kitchenette, tiny bathroom, and a set of bunk beds. These were covered in quilts decorated with Bo-Peeps and clusters of cartoon sheep.

"Sit anywhere."

I glanced around. The one chair, its back carved in an edelweiss pattern, was piled high with magazines. Where exactly was I supposed to sit? Ignoring my plight, you pulled two bottles of beer from the miniature fridge, then rummaged around in a suitcase, finally fishing out a rectangular box.

You stared at the loaded chair. "We'll have to sit on the bunk. Mind your head." Your voice was terse, teacher-like. We perched side by side on the edge of the lower berth while you prodded the lid off the box, beer bottle wedged between your knees. You selected a slide.

I was surprised: I guess I expected you would have dragged your paintings up here.

When you held the transparency up to the light I saw that your hand was trembling violently.

My God, I realized, he's more scared than I am.

We spent the next hour squinting at dozens of slides of your paintings. You seemed concerned that I like them, at the same time insisting, "You can't tell a thing about scale and texture from these things."

They were abstractions, which didn't surprise me. Each painting was divided into sections, like coats of arms, or flags of unknown countries.

When I ventured this opinion you looked doubtful. "One day I'll take you to my studio. You have to see their surfaces."

Your studio in Toronto.

I kept waiting for you to make your move. Though we sat very close on the bed and our hands and thighs frequently brushed, you held back.

I began to get not bored exactly, but restless. The scene had stalled. Discreetly, I glanced at my watch then reached up and stretched and tried vainly to contain a yawn. You were talking about the "syntax of the viewing mode" and my brain had had it; I couldn't take in another word. Fatigue gave me the courage I needed.

I reached out and touched the front of your shirt. It seemed an immensely bold act. All I could think was, I'll die if he doesn't respond.

You responded, all right.

It was as if you'd been waiting for a sign. You reached over with your own hand and trailed your fingers down the front of my T-shirt.

At last.

I shivered as your fingers unhurriedly circled my breast and I watched in a kind of trance. The only sound in the room was your breathing, slow and deep. My skin grew nerve endings out of nowhere and when you peeled off my shirt and unhooked the pale blue bra I floated into the unexpected rush of air. Your eyes were half shut. You began to work at the front of your jeans then dropped your hands suddenly.

"You do it."

I reached forward: this was a dive into the center of a dream. My fingers pressed the metal button through its hole and pulled down the zipper.

"Good," you said in a sleepy voice.

The Bo-Peep quilt let out a sigh as we fell back.

◈ 4 ◈

EVERY MONTH, from the time I was eight years old, Father and I drove to the office of *Scope* magazine in Toronto to deliver the puzzle. He was their crossword man ("Just another ink-stained wretch," he liked to boast). He needed this regular reminder that the world was indeed populated by idiots and psychopaths who, if they weren't trying to mow us down with their vehicles, blasted godawful music out of boom boxes, or wore stiff suits and sat in glass towers breathing the same dank air in and out.

"Tomorrow's our day," he'd say, lifting his one white shirt and tweed sports jacket off their hangers.

I loved going to the city — except for the driving part. Dad was so nervous behind the wheel that as the freeways widened and converged during the approach he'd start yelling, "I can't do it! Everything's happening at once!"

"It's okay, Dad, just keep straight."

"What does that sign say?"

"Yonge Street next right."

"Christ!"

"Right lane must exit."

"Jesus!"

His foot rammed the accelerator as we hurtled into the right lane, forcing a black airport limo to swerve. I peeked in the rear-view; the driver was leaning way back in his seat, arms straight ahead, pressing against the wheel.

We would circle the downtown office block half a dozen times while Father cried, "Keep your eyes peeled for a parking spot!"

There never was one. We'd end up going to the city lot in Chinatown and paying ten dollars.

"I don't know why I do this," he grumbled, making sure all the windows and doors were locked. He answered himself. "To remind myself what I'm not missing." He grabbed my hand for the hair-raising tear across University Avenue.

"That's right, mow us down! Better luck next time, buddy!"

The entire southbound lane of cars screeched to a halt as we raced in front of them. I tugged at Father's arm.

"Can't we cross at the lights?"

"That wouldn't be any fun."

The magazine office was on the twelfth floor. Father never said a word as he pressed the elevator button but would go very pale and unbutton his jacket as if he were suddenly hot. When we stepped in and the doors squeezed shut he would let me press 12. Even if the elevator was crowded I could hear his quick shallow breathing. When we cruised to a stop and the doors pulled open — he was first out of there, elbows flying. Later, when I was older, he'd send me up alone to make the delivery, insisting he found the whole business a "terrific bore." I loved the office; it was so clean and white and buzzing with activity. Phones were constantly ringing, copy machines rattled and hummed, and there was a perpetual smell of burnt coffee. This was always offered to us, in Styrofoam cups with little envelopes of sugar just like in a restaurant. It was always someone's birthday and I would be handed a paper plate bending with cake, dense chocolate or hazelnut, completely unlike the virtuous lemon bread we had at home on special occasions. The hallways were broadloomed with a smoke-colored rug that squished underfoot like spring moss, and I always wanted to kick off my shoes and sink my toes in it.

Dad picked up his check from Miss Steeple, scooped his mail from the cubby he shared with the acrostic lady — and off we'd go. First to the Shanghai Gardens for spicy noodles, then to the museum or art gallery. We'd always buy Mother something — a reproduction of an Egyptian mummy from the museum shop or perhaps a set of Group of Seven postcards. Dad liked to get back on the road well before dark. When we didn't manage this it was very dramatic. Since we were driving northwest the sun broke over our windshield like a runny egg.

"I can't see a thing!" He flailed at the window with both hands as we tore down the middle lane of the 401. "Blind as a bat!"

I braced for the crash which, miraculously, never came.

As the freeway narrowed into a highway, then a road, he relaxed visibly. His shoulders, which had been hunched somewhere near his ears, dropped several inches, and he'd even start singing in a voice that switched from tenor to baritone as he ran through the national anthems of a dozen countries.

There was less than a week before you would head back to Toronto, and each moment I spent away from you was excruciating. Life at my own home was banal to the point of nausea; my parents' little routines and aimless chatter grated until I found myself fleeing the cabin at any pretext.

"I've grown beyond them," I told you, and waited for a sympathetic response.

You just looked thoughtful. "I wonder ..."

You, Otto, were the larger world.

Only by inhaling you, cell by cell, would I too leap into the limitless cosmos.

Over the next three days you picked me up at lunchtime in town and we'd buy fried chicken or burgers and drive into the country for a picnic. I'd watch you at these fast food joints, the way you'd talk up the waitresses and counter boys.

"Business pretty good?"

"Not bad, I guess."

"This a summer gig? Back to school in the fall?"

You leaned on the counter, smiling hard.

They'd examine your clothes, the worn denim jacket, the jeans, and smile back. "Yeah. Brutal."

You nodded sympathetically. "Glory days, huh? Bull shit!"

This, coming from the mouth of a full-fledged adult, was disconcerting. At Kentucky Fried Chicken I saw the boy's eyes dart to mine, then yours, narrowing at first, then relaxing. I lingered by the door clutching a thermal bag while the kid talked a streak.

"The principal's a jerk, eh? She calls up my old man? Says I've been smoking up at the depot and I go so what? It's not like school property? Mind your fucking business ..."

He's my age, I thought, pained at the realization.

"Otto ..."

"Be right there." You tapped the boy's wrist. "Take care, man," and left him with his mouth hanging, mid-sentence.

Dashing across the scorched asphalt to the truck I said, "Why do you do that?"

"Do what?" Wide innocent smile.

After eating at some carefully chosen picnic site we'd wipe our fingers, mash all the greasy paper into the bag, and you'd turn to me.

"Well ...?"

I always kept my eyes open; I didn't want to miss a thing. Your face transformed as you began to sink into me. With your eyes closed, all guile, every speck of irony fell away. Your lids were pale and blank, compressing a little more with each second, and when you came, for an instant you seemed racked by pain. The merest twist or flex of my body would bring it on. I learned to hold you, to wait, choose my moment.

After, lying on our backs and facing the sky, we'd talk for hours. You wanted to know about my life growing up at the cabin, about my one and only boyfriend, Casey Doyle, the cadet from Camp Rupert, and how I'd been hauled out of the local school for good at age ten when my father heard the teacher scream in the schoolyard, "*All of youse line up!*"

Never had I had such an attentive listener.

You sucked details from me I didn't know I had: the position of every object in my bedroom; not just the bed and bureau, but the exact arrangement of brush, comb, and mirror, the shoes neatly lined up, the cupboard with the hopelessly warped door, and the photo taped to the mirror frame.

"Photo?" you interrupted. "Of what?"

"Just the cabin. I took it when I was six or seven, with a pinhole camera."

This delighted you. Everything I'd presumed hopelessly banal was transformed by the intensity of your listening. I was handing over the only knowledge I had: the specifics of my life. I rattled on about every thought, hope, and ambition that had ever crossed my mind.

Once you leaned on your elbow so your face was inches from mine and said, "Your inner and outer lives are perfectly integrated."

I stopped talking, suddenly uneasy. Were you saying I was uncomplicated? Transparent? For the first time I thought — I should have held something back.

As the sun began its slow skid westward you would tell me of your travels. You'd been everywhere: Nepal, Greece, Mexico, Nicaragua, India, Afghanistan. Not for you the constricted world of my parents. You had no use for a safe house on a hill. "Safety," you shrugged, "is another word for sleep."

You'd driven over deserts in a Land Rover, slept in a bombed-out hotel in Managua, had your fortune told by an Indian movie star. And you'd never read a travel book in your life.

"If I'm curious — I just go."

Mother feverishly read travel books, especially those written by daring Victorian women who tramped the mountains and deserts of places like Turkistan and Egypt. She preferred the kind of volume with fold-out maps so she could trace the journey with the tip of her finger.

I couldn't bear to think the week would come to an end. One fantasy sustained me: you would invite me to join you in Toronto, in your studio. After all, your wife was out of the picture and I wouldn't take up much space. I wouldn't bother you while you were working. I was a passable cook.

"Carmen," you once remarked, "is a ferociously ambitious woman. I've never met anyone with her drive, her smarts."

Instant seizure of jealousy. It wasn't only the bit about "smarts" that hurt; it was the careless way you spoke the word "woman," a state of being that still swam just out of reach.

We were lying in the woods at the edge of the provincial park. My skirt was hiked to my waist and you were stroking the inside of my thigh. Suddenly the hand darted away, leaving my skin taut with desire.

"I need to make a phone call."

We sped out of the sheltered wood into the tilting sun of late afternoon.

I hadn't seen you in twenty-four hours and the day sprawled interminably. I marched up and down the streets of Rupert pretending to myself that this was what I liked doing, staring into the same sad store windows at stationery, faded Batmobiles, and out-of-date shoes, when I was really scanning the reflection for any sign of your truck rumbling down the road. Where the hell were you? It was Thursday and you were set to go home the next day. The reality of this deadline had finally penetrated. There had been no mention of me going with you, not a hint.

"It'll be weird here without you," I'd said more than once, thinking I was being subtle. You smiled blandly in response.

Lunch hour had come and gone with no sign of Molly rattling up the street. My stomach growled and I was getting crazier by the minute, imagining you'd snuck off without a word. What was I but a most peripheral part of your existence? For you had a "life," a complex fabric that shadowed you constantly and contained your every gesture. You'd let me in for a time, offered me a segment, but didn't you tell me you intended to "strip down," to "simplify"? Was that a warning? Was there to be no final scene, nothing for me to remember and weep over — and finally feel brave about? Then, as I stood at the corner of Main and South Streets, your truck approached.

And rolled right past.

"Otto!" I waved both arms over my head. You must have spotted me. When you slowed down for the intersection I raced to catch up.

"Otto!" I hammered the side of the truck. Pride wasn't an issue.

You lowered the window. "What's up?" Your face looked awful, white and strained, bags under the eyes.

"I saw the truck ..."

"Hop in." You sounded weary and resigned.

We drove in near silence. You offered no explanation for your drive-by and the missing lunch and I didn't ask. Perhaps I didn't want to know. I sat in the cab while you dashed into the post office, the bank, and finally Canadian Tire. You came back from this last errand hefting a bag, which you pitched into the back seat.

"Know what's in there?"

I didn't.

"One of those big food coolers." Your mood seemed to have changed. You floored the accelerator and screeched out of the parking lot onto the highway.

"Sounds pretty good, doesn't she?" You rapped the dashboard. "I had the hood up all day getting her prepped. Purrs like a housecat; she's ready to go anywhere."

So that's what you'd been doing.

"Toronto isn't exactly the Amazon," I pointed out.

Your left knee jiggered up and down. You were humming.

"Where are we going now?" I said.

You'd steered onto a concession road.

"To the cliffs. To the top of the world for one last look! What do you say, Simone — shall we shoot for the Big E?"

The Big E.

Eternity.

I flashed on an image of the truck dangling over the edge of the cliff, then positioned my hand on the door handle, just in case. I really thought you might do it, Otto. Not because of the pain of losing your wife, but because you'd suddenly decided to experience the "total collapse of will."

(Three days later we'd be barreling down a highway when you swerved toward the line of telephone poles. "Believe in perspective?" you cried. "The vanishing line to infinity?")

"I made a decision," you said. We were sitting on a rock. You'd parked — perfectly conventionally — in the space provided by Parks and Rec. The rock was limestone and covered with initials etched by the youth of Rupert.

"Which is?"

"I'm not going back to Toronto."

"You're not." I straightened.

"I'm driving south, to Mexico."

"Mexico?"

There was an odd hopped-up quality to your voice. You attacked your cigarette with short hard puffs, and threw it down before it was finished.

"I can't hang around my wife's door begging to be let in like some homeless tomcat. I've called my dealer and he can front me some cash. The National Gallery's hot to buy one of the 'Emblem' paintings. And I know a guy who'll sublet the studio." You slapped your knee. "I'm going to fucking go on the road, Simone!"

What was I supposed to do? Pump your hand, wish you luck, a good journey, then stroll back down the hill to my so-called life?

From the cliff I could see smoke loop up from our chimney and hang in the windless air. It was Thursday, baking day. Usually I helped.

You grabbed my hand and pressed it into your chest.
"What do you think?"
I decided to be brave, that this was what you expected.
"Of course I'm sad to hear you're going so far..."
"Sad? Really?" You stared into my eyes.
"But I understand how tough it's been..."
"Do you? Do you really understand? Do you have any idea how much I want to believe that?" You kept staring.
"I just wish —"
"Yes?"
There was a few seconds of silence, then you dropped my hand.
"My God, Simone — what are we going to do?"
I didn't answer; I couldn't.
"Don't you see — I have so little to offer you."
"That's ridiculous!" I came to life. "You've already given me so much."
"Have I?" A slow thoughtful look crept over your face. Reaching out, you took my hand again and placed it between yours, gently rubbing the pulse on my wrist.
"You could come too."
My body went rigid: a crow swept down past your shoulders, spying a crust on the ground.
"You can't stick around here forever," you went on. "You're just starting to blossom."
Blossom. Yes.
"Well?"

A grin smoked across my face. "Well what?"

"Do we know why the dinosaurs died out?"

"Sure, give me a minute. It's because —"

"Their brains were too small."

Right, I was about to say that.

Father remembered everything he read: the dates of Mozart's birth and death, the pattern of drainage in the Amazon Basin, the terms used in Gothic architecture. His brain was fully porous, a miracle-fiber sponge that retained every fact that came within swiping distance.

"Did you know that we lose on average 245 hairs each day?" He pushed his glasses over his nose and peered around the room. "Isn't that marvelous?"

He exclaimed over a new fact the way another man might weep over a line in a Yeats poem.

I stared at both parents when they weren't looking, trying to imagine what it would be like not to be here. Sometimes I was seized by an ache of loneliness, a yawning door that needed only the slightest prod to fling open. Oblivious to all this, they continued their routines: darting in and out of the cabin with fistfuls of lettuce and chives from the garden, filling the stove with firewood, and hauling the day's mail from the bottom of the hill. Father set his knife and a pocketful of coins on the table before dragging the old tin tub onto the grass for his ritual shampoo and bath. He loved perching there on the scrabbly field, soaping himself, singing the great tenor arias, lunging for notes he couldn't hope to reach.

"*Figaro! Figaro! Fiii-garo!*"

"Facts?" You shrugged your shoulders with indifference. "Just another mode of viewing the world, the great hierarchy of reason. The true challenge is to embrace chaos!"

Chaos — yes. The word was fraught with risk and danger, the shining boulder of kryptonite.

What I'd forgotten is how close it had been. If I hadn't waited around the main street of Rupert that day, clinging for hours to its hot dusty pavement, would you have simply started driving south without me?

Would you have glided from town in your freshly aligned wheels, the new cooler bumping across the back seat, telling yourself it was all for the best? That, after all, you had so little to offer.

"I was thinking of going somewhere." My lips were dry.

Mother's hand reached inside the chicken and removed the kidneys. "Where?"

Father glanced up from the Random House atlas.

"I've been invited to go to Mexico."

"Mexico!" He slammed the book shut.

"With whom?" Mother said calmly.

"Otto Guest."

"Terrific." Father started coughing, a sure sign that he was distressed.

"On what terms are you being invited?" Mother's tone remained unflustered.

"What's that supposed to mean?" Suddenly I was annoyed. What right had they to quiz me on my plans? "If you mean, are we lovers — of course we are."

All activity in the room froze. Mother stared at me, one hand still resting inside the pimply-fleshed chicken.

"I thought this character was married," Dad gasped between coughs.

"He is, nominally."

"Nominally?" His eyebrows shot up.

"His wife left him a couple of weeks ago."

"Great."

"Perhaps —" Mother began.

"How old is he," Father interrupted, "this unwelcome Guest?"

I pretended to think. "Forty ... five."

They'd known something was up, of course, with my frequent unexplained absences and distracted air. There was much talk in our household of making one's own way in life without being swayed by the pack. Father despised all authority figures, from cops to teachers to parking-lot attendants.

"You can't go," he said.

"What do you mean?" I was indignant. "Of course I can."

Mother set a hand on his shoulder and I saw the tips of her fingers dig in. "What are you going to do, Frank, tie her to the bedpost?"

"For Pete's sake, the guy's my age nearly, and married."

"He's got a son," I added. I was half enjoying this.

"A middle-aged married man with a kid. Terrific." He shook off my mother and started pacing the room. I could smell his panic. The world had invaded his safe house on the hill, the lunatic world he'd managed to keep at bay. He smacked his hands against his thighs and looked out the window. Was this just the beginning? Were "they" coming? Had the raid begun? I almost felt sorry for him. At the same time I was determined to hold my ground.

"It was a mistake to send you to that damn summer school. Who do these teachers think they are? Your brain isn't enough? Now he wants your body?"

I had to laugh. "You make it sound so science fiction."

"And Mexico." He threw up his hands.

"What's wrong with Mexico?"

"It's the third world, that's what's wrong."

"A developing nation," Mother corrected. She turned to me and said, with an effort at a casual tone, "They have diseases there: cholera, malaria, probably dengue fever. It's not like here."

"I know. That's why I want to go."

"You don't speak a word of the language."

A desperate ploy. I began to get angry again. It was their fear that annoyed me; I was afraid it might be contagious.

"All either of you do is read about places. You know the facts about cities, what the population is, the gross national product, the percentage of live births — but you're terrified to set foot on foreign soil. You're both ruled by fear!"

Father's chin dropped and for once he didn't answer.

"I'm not afraid," Mother said quietly. "I'd go anywhere."

Suddenly she was sitting at the kitchen table pulling a card out of the recipe index. "We'll have this Otto up for lunch. Isn't that the thing to do, Frank? Tomorrow at one. We can pick some of that asparagus before the rabbits finish it off."

That night I went to my bedroom early. I couldn't stand the dour silence in the room, the sharp accusing looks. Father would draw a breath as if about to say something, then drop his magazine. Mother, on full alert, faced him down with a stare.

I lay on the bed, heart pounding, lurching between excitement and bone-chilling fear. I wished you were there, that I could reach out and remind myself you existed.

There was a knock on the door.

"Come in."

Dad perched on the edge of my desk (made from two rain barrels and a piece of plywood) and folded his arms. His hair, what was left of it, stuck straight up in the air as if he'd been running his hands through it.

"This is crazy," he said.

"What is?" I stuffed a pillow under one shoulder.

"This so-called plan of yours."

I felt myself harden. "I don't think it's crazy."

"Who *is* this guy?" His face reddened and I could feel him counting, forcing the blood pressure down. "Who the hell is he?"

"An artist. And I love him."

I was glad you weren't listening: the word "love" had never cropped up in our conversations. I found myself glancing out the window, just to make sure you weren't standing with an ear pressed to the pane.

"For Pete's sake, Simone, how could you think he'd —"

"He'd what?" My voice was icy.

Dad slipped off the desk and stood there in my bedroom, not knowing what to do with his hands, jabbing them in and out of his pockets and dislodging little shreds of Kleenex. "I'm asking you not to go."

I just shrugged. Of course I would go. I had to. I didn't want to become this frightened person, squirreled away on the fringes of the world.

It might work. I imagined Father crouched forward on the edge of his chair, glasses pushed over his nose as you spoke. He would interrupt often, deliberately not following the conversation.

"Define 'simulacra' for this unenlightened party."

And you would ask how things had been made, even slipping under the table to view the elaborate trestle that tilted three ways. After lunch, which would be delicious, you would turn to me and demand to see the outhouse.

The toilet with its pagoda roof modeled on a Shinto temple, and the louvered door that always stuck.

"The folks want to take a look at you." My tone was light, so you wouldn't guess how much it meant to me.

"I bet they do."

We'd just stepped out of the Rupert Family Clinic and were rolling down our sleeves. We'd had shots for diseases I'd barely heard of.

"Mom's offered to make lunch tomorrow."

You said nothing but wrapped your arm tightly around mine as we crossed the street to the parked truck. I felt my skin pulse where the needle had gone in.

I asked again, before we parted for the night, adopting the same breezy tone.

"So, are you up for it tomorrow?"

You looked puzzled. "Up for what?"

"Lunch."

"Ah yes." You lazily pushed the package of maps back onto the dashboard. We were parked at the foot of my hill, motor idling, recovering from a long goodbye kiss. Your eyes were still half shut, your breath soft and quick.

"What time?" Your lids fluttered open.

"One o'clock."

The next morning I was pressed into service, sweeping the floor, dusting, picking asparagus, baking sourdough rolls. The only time we ever had guests was when the aunts and cousins visited.

"Does your friend smoke?"

I allowed that you did. Mother placed an ashtray on the rickety coffee table. This gesture was enough to give the cabin an exotic air. Surreptitiously I removed a painted chestnut-in-bird's-nest thing I'd made the summer before. I replaced it with one of my drawings from class, held down with a rock. I'd already stowed — weeks ago — the overwrought surrealist paintings.

"Do you think it's going to rain?" Mother parted the curtains and looked out at the bay.

"Those are cirrostratus clouds, unlikely to contain precipitation." Father didn't bother looking up from his work. He was feeding the ants in his ant farm, an aquarium filled with sand and gravel and glass tubing. He was trying to breed a super race, blending tiny red ants the local librarian had smuggled back from Costa Rica with a local species.

I went outside to pump a pail full of water, and while water streamed over my bare feet, I gazed down toward the highway. An orange school bus roared by, its windows open and full of tiny smiling faces.

One o'clock came and went. Unsurprised, Father plunked down in his chair to finish drawing up the month's puzzle. Most of his crosswords took on a subject, like ornithology or the decline of the British Empire. This month, judging by the books piled at his feet, the topic was the Crusades.

I glanced furtively out the window. Nothing. Faint sound of traffic buzzing by on the highway below. Where were you?

"There's no phone here," I said aloud. "No way to get hold of us."

There was a sharpness in my voice.

"I can't leave this soufflé in the oven a second longer." Mother reached into the stove with fat mitts on her hands, and the smell of crispy cheese and butter filled the room.

Not a whisper of blame or indignation. No reference at all to the missing guest.

The egg and cheese oozed perfectly as we cut into the soufflé. Conversation took the form of short remarks punctuated by long tense silences. The crazy part was I was angry at them for what I imagined they were thinking.

How dare they judge you?

How dare they contain you within the rules of their tiny universe?

You spied me later that afternoon as I emerged from the municipal offices after delivering a check for property taxes — three months late.

"Simone!" You waved a slim white envelope. "It came!"

"What came?"

You threaded your way between a Tasty Freeze truck and the Rupert tourist kiosk. "The check from Benny. Ten grand. We're set up." You sought my hand to high-five.

I didn't respond, keeping both arms clamped firmly to my sides.

"What's wrong?"

"We missed you today." I watched your face as it passed from puzzlement to wincing recognition.

"Are you very angry with me?"

"Should I be?"

A station wagon with New Jersey plates drove up to the tourist kiosk. The girl leaned over the counter to pass the driver, a man with a broad pink face, two brochures: "Rupert: Apple Country" and "Colony Bay: Home of the Great Trout Race."

"I hope you'll apologize to your folks — on my behalf." I waited.

"The thing is —" You propped one foot on the guardrail. "I've been so filled with your stories of them, so soaked with images of your life on the hill, that I guess I didn't want to spoil it."

My eyebrows lifted. "Spoil what?"

"Don't you see? You've created a sort of mythology that is rich and seamless — and utterly complete." Your eyes locked on the tourist's car as it sped away. "Ever read a book and loved it — then made the mistake of going to see the movie?"

"Sure."

Finally you looked at me. "So you understand."

☀ 5 ☀

YOU WERE TO PARK at the foot of the hill at dawn. The suitcase dug into my thigh as I tramped down the slope. They were watching, of course. Hadn't I deliberately let the door snap shut behind me? I felt how each step downhill would alter the trajectory of their stare. I was proud of this image; it seemed like something you would think of.

You leaned over to unlock the door.

"Hi," I said gravely.

Your hand scurried up my cheek. "Sure about this?"

"Of course."

As the highway unraveled I perched at the edge of my seat and waited for the rest of my life to begin.

We were together twenty-four hours of the day. That was all I'd ever wanted. Cartons of books bumped around the back seat, and in the evenings when we stopped to eat I'd root around, reading sentences from one then another: Beckett, Pound, Bataille, Ondaatje ... a little short on women but I didn't notice that.

"The twentieth century is unavoidable," you said. "Open your eyes, dear, before it slips away."

This was a heretical notion, that the twentieth century wasn't something to protect oneself from at all costs.

The hours of driving were punctuated with discourses on *arte povera* or the inner life of reptiles — anything that crossed your mind. I fed you opening lines then lapped up every word. Whenever you flagged, I'd toss out another question.

Once you gave me a dark look. "You frighten me sometimes, Simone. Your greed is so absolute; you could suck me dry."

Where Father hunched over the steering wheel, clenching it with both hands, preparing for collision, you leaned back easily, hooked the bottom of the wheel with a thumb, and draped your left arm out the window.

"The young lady?"

"Simone Paris," I answered, leaning over your lap.

The border guard stared at my birth certificate and your passport.

"She's my student." Your voice was crisply professional.

"How long will you be in the United States?"

"Just for the day. We're going to visit the art museum."

This was Buffalo. A cindery smell rose from the tall brick smokestacks. Suddenly there were black people everywhere, unfamiliar license plates, and the guard's voice was full of flattened vowels. I'd never been to the United States. I'd never been anywhere.

The documents were passed back through the open window.

"Enjoy your visit."

"We will." You charged into the right lane.

"We're not really just going for the day?" I said, trying not to sound anxious. Maybe I'd got it all wrong.

"Of course not." You looked at me in surprise.

Glory days!

Your hand drummed on my knee while the radio blasted country-and-western music.

All that I'd been taught to despise — you loved.

Billboards!

Kentucky Fried Chicken!

Fat people!

At dusk we'd cruise around searching for the perfect campsite. Not some banal pine grove — that was no challenge. You'd gaze critically at bridge trestles, dark alleys, landfill sites, until finally you let out a hoot and pulled up next to a deserted factory.

Okay, I give up.

Why this powerfully unattractive stretch of asphalt and stained brick? You pushed in the emergency brake and heaved a sigh of satisfaction.

"See the part of the wall that juts out?"

I followed your outstretched finger. "Yes."

"Must be the elevator shaft. What a queer angle; it skews the whole building."

I squinted, trying to see what you saw.

"Look at the trees behind."

I looked.

"They could almost be floating, an illusion caused by the skewed foreground." You reached for the cooler and yanked out a beer. "Beautiful."

If only I could learn to tune my senses this sharply! I would not sleepwalk through life. I would not mark time with a clothespin pinched on my nose, oven mitts buffering my hands, ears clogged with cotton.

We drove and drove and the landscape buckled and flattened and heaved. Texas opened up and bled land until we were sure there could be none left. Then half the signs were in Spanish and suddenly there were factories everywhere, and wooden shacks, and schools that were plain slabs of concrete. You dropped packages of salty peanuts doused in chili on my lap, and tossed money to children with dark skin. Finally we crossed the second border and the smell of the air changed.

"Livestock, with a hint of rancid cooking oil," you sniffed expertly and cranked up the radio.

"Baby — Heaven sent me you ..."

"Somewhere along here is the turnoff." Father geared down despite traffic streaming on all sides. "I'm counting on you to navigate."

We'd just begun to cross the Bloor Viaduct, a vast concrete bridge that straddles the Don River Valley and leads to east-end Toronto. The turnoff would twist us hundreds of feet below to the seething parkway.

"Suicidal maniac!" Father shouted to the cyclist darting by, clipping our mirror with his handlebar.

I wasn't listening. Instead I watched as a woman, dressed in a neat blue skirt and Liberty cotton blouse, made her way smartly along the sidewalk till she reached the bulge in the center of the bridge. This was a convenient spot to pause and survey the view, a panorama of winding riverbed, trees, skyline, and highway. She looped her purse over her neck, pressed both hands on top of the pebbly railing, and gracefully heaved herself up.

"Oh!" I cried.

"Now?" Dad jerked the wheel sideways. "Are you sure? Can I switch lanes?"

She rose to a standing position, and without a shred of hesitation, stepped forward. Into nothing.

"Stop!" I cried.

"I can't." Dad sounded angry. "Do you want to get us killed? We've missed the damn turnoff and whose fault is that?"

Moments later we pulled out of the firehall where we'd disturbed two burly firemen playing table tennis.

"They didn't seem the least surprised," I repeated for the third time. "As if this happens all the time." I was shaking and my throat was dry.

"It does," Father said. "The city makes them crazy. They jump from bridges, trestles, office towers, scaffolding — any place high enough."

I held the image all day, of bodies raining down on us, legs and arms splayed, mouths open in wordless screams.

Before leaving the firehall I'd made sure they had our address, and I drew a map on a scrap of paper showing how to get to the cabin from the main highway.

"Her family may want to talk to me," I explained, snapping the seatbelt across my chest. "I was the last person to see her alive."

☀ 6 ☀

WE WERE THE only tourists at the beach town. This was a year after the 1985 earthquake, and the bigger hotels that backed into the sea had frozen mid-tilt, their lower floors squashed. As we approached, walking along the beach, I felt dizzy for a minute, before realizing it was the building listing seaward, not me.

Three lines of surf pounded onto an endless sandy beach. There wasn't a soul in sight, not even a fisherman. We fooled about in the waves, wading in then shrieking as a swell chased us back to shore. You'd grab my hand and we charged in and out for hours. I was never afraid.

"This is paradise!" we chimed, faces beet red from the sun.

Paradise wasn't only the ocean that stretched as far as we could see, or the children who laughed when they saw us coming, or the hotel with its courtyard and dry fountain and the big empty restaurant — it was the fact I had you all to myself.

"Race you to the Coke stand!" You rolled up your pants to the knees, kicked off your runners, and started down the sand. I was hot on your tail, yet not too hot, for I'd learned to let you win. The one time I'd swept by easily you immediately braked and bent over, huffing and grabbing your chest. "You're too damn young for me, Simone!"

Each day when we woke up there would be a plan: "We'll hire a boat to take us to Monkey Island" or "Let's lie in bed all day: I'll read to you."

Our room was on the second floor of La Tropicana, a small, blazing-white stucco hotel. As we drove up to it you'd scanned the foundations with a suspicious eye, looking for cracks. "If there are any," you decided, popping open the door of the truck, "they've plastered them over so we can't see."

We were at the end of the hall, overlooking the courtyard on one side and the sea on the other. The Pacific Ocean. The room itself was bare, except for the bed with its bright orange spread, and a single wooden chair pushed against the wall. Above, a fan languidly turned its blades, cutting through the torpor of midday haze.

At mealtimes we had the restaurant to ourselves, although each table was carefully laid out with cloth napkins, cutlery, and heavy blue china plates. The proprietors, a middle-aged couple, often ate at a corner table, leaving the daughter to cook and the three sons to act as waiter, maître d', and busboy.

"Smell!" we'd cry upon awakening each morning. Our open window tugged in the salty spray.

"Taste!" you'd grin, biting into a freshly caught curl of squid, its flesh glistening with garlic oil.

I felt your eyes follow all my movements; as I rose from the bed to stand by the window, or when I crossed the floor of the patio carrying icy bottles of Carta Blanca. Sometimes you'd urge me to walk a few feet ahead on the beach and I knew it was because you wanted to watch the swing of my hips.

I was coated by your desire, slick with it, and could imagine no other way to exist.

Then one afternoon, during siesta, you remarked calmly, "We don't have to spend every second together."

We were sprawled crossways on the orange bedspread while above, the ceiling fan skipped hot air over our naked bodies.

"We don't?" I stiffened.

"You could go for a walk all on your own."

So then of course I had to. I slipped into my thongs, tank top, hat and shorts and hiked twenty minutes in midday heat down the beach in a purposeful stride. Was that long enough? Sweat streamed down my back and between my breasts. I didn't see anything; not the ocean or sky, or the dogs yapping around a fish carcass. The thatched-roof hut where we'd sat so many times at sunset, drinking rum, was invisible. My eyes were stupid, unable to enter the world. I remembered reading of a woman who'd lost her sense of taste and how she'd come to despise eating. Were you still napping, or were you standing on the balcony in your shorts, looking down, wondering if that speck on the beach was me? Suddenly I was seeing myself — the tiny darting figure — from your perspective, and for that instant I became visible again.

I sprinted back to the hotel and tore up the stairs, leaving little sprays of sand underfoot.

The room was empty. Just for a second, I panicked. Then I spied your knapsack and the copy of Prévert's *Paroles* fanned on the bed. You couldn't have gone too far. I listened for the sound of the shower crashing on tile. Nothing. Then I saw the note, scrawled on a sheet of airmail paper.

I'M IN THE BAR.

The letters were oversize, taking up the whole page.

I splashed some water over my face, toweled off, then dashed back down the grainy steps. I knew which bar you meant, the one in the fancy hotel half a mile down the beach, decked out with bougainvillea and a turquoise swimming pool.

You were hunched over at our usual table. An empty Carta Blanca stood at the edge of the tablecloth and you were well into a second. The bar was otherwise empty. You must have whipped down here the moment I left. Then I saw your address book on the table, held open by a dish of peanuts. Perhaps you had been writing postcards, although I saw no evidence of this. I was seized by another thought — that you had come here to use the long-distance phone, the only one in town.

But who would you be calling? Benny, your dealer?

"You weren't gone long." You shut the little book and slipped it into your pocket. I tried not to rest my eyes there. You pulled out a chair. "Good to get off on your own?"

"Sure," I lied. Your face seemed to have altered slightly. It was that forty minutes of unaccounted-for time; I'd missed the tiny gradations that move us from second to second. It was disconcerting, like walking into a movie that's already under way.

"I went to the —"

"Shhh." You held up a hand. "I don't need to know where you went. There's such a thing as —" you hesitated — "private life."

My hand reached for the peanuts.

"*Una margarita para la señorita,*" you recited for the waiter, a stiff young man in a slightly soiled uniform.

Driving through northern Mexico you'd told me the story of a young monk who arrived at the temple of the Zen master, begging to be taken in. "Roshi shut the door on the poor fuck. The young monk, seeing this as a test of his devotion, sat on the icy stone steps for a week, without food or drink. One day, when Roshi swung open the door, he nearly tripped over the guy. 'Ah, it's you,' the master said. 'Why didn't you knock?' "

You found this tale hilarious — and instructive. I laughed uneasily. Was I supposed to be the young monk? Had I not found the way to knock?

We drank and listened to water cascade down the elaborate fountain. There was a plaster fish with an open mouth that gushed seawater onto a series of widening platters. After a second margarita I relaxed and we started to play our favorite game, inventing Spanish words for everyday objects. I had you stumped with "*bomba de corno*" when a sound, at once foreign and utterly familiar, made us both look up. A middle-aged gringo couple were descending the stairs from the upper tier of rooms. We hadn't seen tourists in over a week.

"I like facing the ocean," the woman said. "I like the sound."

"It keeps me awake," the man grumbled, "and my damn leg's still stiff."

"If you didn't scramble to the top of every ruin in sight ..."

Then she saw us.

You raised your bottle in greeting. She waved a brightly flowered sleeve back and chirped, "*Buenas tardes,*" while behind, the husband gave a pinched smile.

I felt an immediate pang of dismay; paradise had been invaded and the sound of the invaders' English fouled the air.

"Care to join us for a drink?" you said.

"Otto," I muttered.

The woman tucked her hand under her husband's elbow and steered him to our table. Her breasts bobbed under the gaily printed blouse.

"Thank God," she said, "we've only had each other to talk to since Zee."

"Which was yesterday," her husband pointed out. Up close I saw he had a thin blond mustache.

His name, it turned out, was Derek, and he was a semi-retired engineer from Albany.

"I'm Trisha," she extended her hand. "College teacher back home."

"Oh yes?" you smiled encouragingly. "Of what?"

"Marketing strategies for small business."

Did you wince? Not at all. On the contrary, you couldn't have made her feel more welcome. Direct marketing was the most interesting topic in the world, one would think, listening to your stream of questions. She basked in the attention, slipping her hand behind her neck and loosening her hair.

"Do you have them do field work?" you wondered. "Develop their own product campaigns?"

"You bet." She was well into a piña colada, sinking her teeth into the chunk of rum-drenched pineapple. "They invent their own product and devise a market for it. Create need and desire."

"Need and desire," you repeated, and glanced meaningfully at the rest of us. "Isn't that what we always try and evoke in each other?"

Derek, who was sitting next to me, squirmed and cleared his throat. He smelled of coconut oil and pipe tobacco.

"We're not run-of-the-mill tourists," Trisha confided later. "We like to get off the beaten track. How else do you discover the soul of a country?"

"I agree completely." Then you slid your elbows toward the center of the table and rested your cheek on your hands. Your eyes were level with her Elizabeth Taylor breasts, which swelled above her blouse in two plump, tanned mounds. Between them the skin glistened with sweat, and when she drew a deep breath in the midst of her chatter, they rose magnificently, pressing against the skimpy, fuchsia colored cloth.

Evidently she didn't mind your staring, for she took every opportunity to bend forward and give you a full, unobstructed look.

You couldn't keep your eyes off her, Otto. You were transfixed by those two freckled mounds. Derek and I tried our own little stabs at conversation but it was pointless. He looked miserable and tired, as if this were all too familiar.

I ordered another drink, my third.

I waited for you to say, "Haven't you had enough?" But you didn't notice the waiter setting a new glass on the table. I picked up a corner of the napkin and rubbed the coarse salt from the rim. My lips were stinging from the mixture of lime and salt and alcohol.

Her hand dropped on your wrist. "Derek and I decided we need to recharge our marriage. The grind of jobs, kids, mortgage, and whatnot can really wear down the edges, if you know what I mean."

Then, for the first time, she glanced my way. Her smile was brittle. "I see you have found your own solution."

I reddened.

Your hand reached across the table and clamped over mine. "This young lady," you announced, "is saving my life."

She looked at me intently and nodded, like she knew exactly what you meant. My skin went cold and you must have felt it, for you began to massage my hand between yours. Then you leaned over and whispered something into her ear. Trisha stared into the center of the table, as if considering, then whispered back.

Your hands continued to rub mine, back and forth, up and down.

Suddenly we were all on our feet, stumbling against the heavy wooden furniture and pulling out peso bills.

"I hope we run into each other again," you said in a stagy voice.

"I'm sure we will," Trisha laughed and wrapped an arm around her husband's waist. "This place isn't exactly Rome, or Cairo."

We were so drunk the sand seemed to grab at our ankles.

"Women like that ..." you began.

"Like what?" I said.

"Who think they can 'recharge' a marriage, plug it in for a week or two and get enough juice to last another decade." You snorted. "What crap. And how sad, how very very sad."

It was getting dark and the beach was cool. For the first time since our arrival we'd missed the sunset. You shivered and pulled me in tight to your hip. Some animal — probably a rat — skittered under one of the huts.

"Don't take history too seriously. It's just one locus of possibility. We can't prove the world existed a week ago, let alone thousands of years."

"Wait a minute, Otto; there's fossils, carbon dating — yesterday's newspaper!"

You waved this objection aside. "Perhaps the whole works was conceived this instant. History, simultaneous with the present."

Spasm of vertigo. I grabbed at the notion, scared yet excited.

But now I wonder: was this just your way of worming out of causality?

I didn't fall asleep that night. What happened is only what I expected. After hours of staring at the white stucco wall, watching a platoon of tiny red ants head from the floor to a crack in the ceiling, I heard, then felt you slip out of bed. Carefully, you laid the sheet back across my naked body. Then you pulled on your clothes, tugged the door open as quietly as possible, then paused a moment. Perhaps you were looking at my form under the sheet, checking the rhythm of my breathing. Was she asleep? I forced the air out in long, deep exhalations. The door shut with a hollow clink and I listened as your bare feet skittered down the steps into the courtyard.

You'd gone for a smoke.

If that was the case, why didn't you just push open the glass door and step out onto the balcony? You'd done that before, when you couldn't sleep. I'd wake up, smelling nicotine, and reach across in the darkness, feeling the empty sag in the bed where you had been.

This time I didn't get up. Instead, I rolled to the center of the bed, where the mattress still had some firmness, and waited for you to return.

This woman you were meeting — I couldn't compete with her lush body, her knowing look, the crow's-feet that sprayed from the corners of her eyes. I lay rigidly, sweating despite the overhead fan, and forced myself to imagine it all. I was there with you on the dark beach burrowing into the fine, soft sand: I was your hand fondling her huge breasts, I was the flick of your tongue on her half-shut eyes. And I was your hand when it slid under her skirt and stroked the smooth, tanned skin. She moaned and let her legs fall open. When your fingers moved in and out, my own hand pressed under the sheet between my slick thighs, in and out.

We drove down the Pacific coast, visiting one resort after another. Paradise never lasted more than two or three days. I'd wake up in the morning to find you sitting on the edge of the bed with the map unfolded and a concentrated look on your face.

"See this?" You'd prod a dot on a tiny peninsula. "Bet Cortés and the boys never set foot near the place."

Enthusiasm flew back into your body. Once, after three days in a tiny unpronounceable fishing village, you pressed your fingers to your temples.

"Why am I doing this? I feel like I'm on the lam."

We were sitting in the shade of one of those beach huts that serve fried shrimp drenched in garlic.

"Why, Simone?"

Seconds earlier, sipping rum from a hairy coconut shell, feet sifting through the sand, I'd allowed myself to sigh with pure happiness.

Now you shifted on the rickety bench and reached into the back pocket of your shorts for your wallet.

"This is my son."

You knocked out two slightly damp Polaroids onto the table.

"Kip."

I looked. The first picture showed a boy of perhaps twelve standing on a beach, wearing baggy trunks and a T-shirt, mugging for the camera. He was swinging a piece of kelp over his head like a lasso. His legs were very long and thin.

"That was in Tofino," you said. "We had a little trailer parked on the sand one summer. Look at him." You poked the edge of the photograph. "Seen a happier kid?"

I nodded no.

The other picture was more recent. The boy was indoors, hunched over a table, wearing an expression just short of a scowl. It was the same face, but older; the cheekbones were harder, the chin more pronounced, and he had long straggly hair. His eyes were pinpoints of reflected red light.

"Three months ago," you said softly. "Know what he was saying as I snapped this? "Fuck off, Dad." Know what I did? Took seven shots more. Finished off the roll — ping-ping-ping — and they all look identical. Kid didn't move a muscle."

7

THE CLOUDS WERE BUILDING, casting shadows over the surface of the bay. I fastened the binoculars to my eyes just as the first rumble of thunder rolled in from the northeast.

He wouldn't try it in this weather.

Sure he would. Didn't I know this boy inside out?

Nicky Peel lifted his bike down the front steps and pointed it toward the highway. It had already started raining. There was a growl of thunder overhead. He wasn't wearing a jacket but it was too late to go back now. He pumped down Main Street, the three blocks it took to leave town. The last of Rupert flashed by, the clapboard houses, the stores with their windows full of useless junk covered in amber plastic. He raced past the town sign, his shirt steaming from dampness and sweat, up toward the escarpment. Overhead the clouds rolled in.

By the time he reached the top of the path the storm hit full force. He could barely see a dozen feet ahead, and when he ditched the bicycle just short of the cliff and stared down, the lake was a gray haze.

Only an idiot would decide to go for a swim in this weather.

He couldn't even see what was rock and what was water; everything had turned the same shade of gray.

He pulled off his shirt and jeans. He'd done this a million times; he could do it with his eyes shut. As the rain pelted his skin he felt his way to the edge of the cliff.

When he hit water it was an explosion of cold, and first he was sure he'd done it, smashed his head open, but after a few seconds he realized it was just the shock of the storm-swollen water against his sweaty skin. He couldn't see a fucking thing. The swells pumped him along and when he twisted to figure out where he was, there were no cliffs, no shoreline, no nothing.

He clawed at the water and yelled, "Hey!"

When people drown they bloat, then burst when the sun hits them. Guts all over the place! Sal and Griffen would be poking around the dock and find him jammed against the tires, a stinking mess, feet wrapped in weeds. Touch him with a stick and — bam! He'd spew in all directions.

Then he saw something looming ahead, a darker tone than the surroundings, like a sub coming up for air. The cliff! He was laughing! Eyes snagged to that bulge of shoreline, he went at it, arms and legs beating the water till he was skimming over top. Nicky, Torpedo Man.

PART TWO

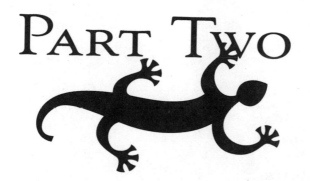

 **8**

"WE SHOULD HAVE DONE this weeks ago. Feel your ears pop? That's the brain cracking open." You floored the accelerator as we crept up the mountain road. "This dirt's residue of glacial sweep, can you imagine ... *hey!*"

A yellow bus had hurtled around the turn and was barreling toward us right down the center of the narrow road.

"Otto!" My hands gripped the dashboard while one foot pumped an imaginary brake. A cloud of dust shot through the open window. It seemed to take forever before you reacted. The bus driver leaned on his horn, blaring the opening phrase of "Battle Hymn of the Republic," and I could see him hunched over the wheel, white shirt billowing, black hair combed smooth, mouth set in a determined line.

Finally you lurched the wheel to the right.

A scant inch of hard-baked earth separated us from the edge of the cliff. I leaned forward, cautiously, as if the shift in weight might send us careening over. Two hundred feet below was a cluster of wooden crosses planted on mounds of

dirt: three big ones, four little ones. I turned, about to say
"Didn't you see it coming?" — but you were slumped over the
wheel, shoulders heaving like you'd sprinted a mile.

"Otto?" My voice sounded funny.

"Otto?" I touched the back of your neck.

You lifted your head and I saw that your eyes were
red, your cheeks wet. You squinted down at the makeshift
cemetery. "Doesn't take much, no sir," then you gripped the
stick shift and wrestled it into reverse.

"There she is!" A hand slapped my padded knee. I'd tugged a
blanket over my sleeveless dress as we drove further from the
tropical coast. The air was cool and sharp now, each breath
defined. This was an entirely different world; long vanished
were the lush palms, the sleepy air dense with humidity and
sea smells, birds of flamboyant plumage. This landscape had
a restrained palette: earth tones with brittle bushes and mud-
colored huts lit by a sweeping, radiantly blue sky.

We'd begun, at last, to coast downhill.

"San Patricio?"

"Right you are, dear."

Excitement popped back into my cramped body. I
stretched goose-pimpled legs as far as they'd go and linked
my fingers, cracking the knuckles. We coasted into a long
shallow valley, between the folds of dung-colored mountains.
I yawned and felt my ears pop and suddenly could hear
music from a distant radio. A dozen church spires cast bony
shadows while a rosy light shimmied off what was, as you'd
promised — a lake. Water. An improbable sight in this
parched, brick-toned landscape. You gave a whoop as the
truck picked up speed while I perched on the edge of the seat,
heart racing. San Patricio; you'd been talking about this place
for days, ever since that last evening in the tiny hamlet where
we'd pitched our hammocks and got eaten alive by outsize
mosquitoes.

"This is a magical place, Simone. Transforming."

Transforming? From what into what? And why did the notion make me uneasy? I gripped the dashboard so my skull wouldn't thwack the roof as we clattered downhill.

("What is color?"

A pause. "Light?" I ventured.

"And the perception of light. Never forget process, dear."

You touched my eyelids then swept your hand up to my scalp.

"Always eye and brain together, Simone; the A team.")

San Patricio was a moderately pretty town; a cluster of Colonial buildings framed the main plaza, and the cathedral was an oddball specimen with a Baroque front, a Gothic add-on, and an open square to the side. But secretly I thought we'd driven through more interesting and picturesque places along the way.

We braked outside a crumbling monastery.

"See that?" You pointed to the facade, stucco that had been cracked, mended, and cracked again. "Peckertracks from a hundred earthquakes. This is a place that never forgets where it's been." You scrambled out of the car.

Earthquakes? Tentatively I set my feet on the ground, half expecting it to yawn open.

"Suck in a lungful of tasty mountain air!" Your chest gave a vigorous heave. "This town is stronger than memory; it has, thank God, a life of its own." You were racing now toward the main square, hauling my arm out of its socket.

"Not so fast!" I scampered to keep up. "The altitude!" I could feel my heart jigger against my ribcage.

You just laughed. "This oxygen is the straight goods, no extra molecules, stripped-down. Look —" You stopped long enough to point. "The hardware store, Don Benito's, and there's Las Flores where I drank gritty coffee. And, Jesus ..." You froze. "Beto?"

"Beto?" I repeated, squinting into the opening of the restaurant. A waiter was removing a basket of rolls from a table, his uniform jacket straining across his bulky shoulders.

"Must be the son," you muttered. "He was just a kid then, used to practice English on us."

"Us?" I said, instantly wary.

"I bet he has half a dozen kids of his own by now."

"Us" could be generic, of course, meaning "all us gringos," except something had softened in your face, as if the memory were specific and somehow sad.

"I'm afraid to speak to him."

"Afraid?" I said. "Why?"

"In case he's forgotten me."

I started to laugh, then saw you weren't kidding. You kept patting the sides of your pants, sliding your hands up and down.

"Time," you said finally. "Where does it all go?"

I listened for a trace of self-mockery, a sneer at your own banality, but heard none. Embarrassed, I stared beyond your shoulder, right into the face of a young soldier standing guard outside the Banamex. His submachine gun rested casually between his thighs as he lit a cigarette. Our eyes met for a second, then suddenly he leaned back and began talking to someone in the doorway of the bank. A girl, dressed in a flowered dress and plastic sandals.

"I translated a letter for his father once," you went on in the same voice. "From some people in California where he worked every summer ..."

The plaza was framed by crumbling sixteenth-and seventeenth-century buildings, their walls bleached white except for strips of red along the bottom. Along two sides the porticoes provided shade for the vendors of comic books and cheap watches and bootleg cassette tapes. An ancient crone sat on a low stool selling homemade tamales from a bucket. A few feet away a man sold boiled corn on the cob from a vast bin out in the sun. An open tub of mayonnaise, seething with bacteria, sat next to the jars of hot sauce. Children lined up for water at a public tap, carrying plastic buckets, politely waiting their turn. This architecture was austere, even somber, and the foliage, such as it was, drooped in the afternoon sun. I bet there'd been no rain for months. The air was so dry my tongue kept running over my parched lips and when I swallowed, something stuck halfway. I popped a Vicks lozenge — a lemony sweetness I will forever link with San Patricio.

You let out another cry. "The ice cream joint!" and we tore across the plaza, weaving between wrought-iron benches and the fountain, past candy sellers and shoeshine boys, until we reached the sign saying NIEVES, with its crudely painted picture of an ice cream cone.

"We'd come here all the time."

Us. We. Were you consciously dropping clues? Yet when I checked your face, your expression was guileless, filled only with excitement and recognition.

A man cut in front of us, leaning into a cart piled high with burlap sacks.

"Watch it!" You pressed a hand against my chest.

The bags wiggled furiously, threatening to overturn the cart, and a pig snout poked through an opening, honking for air.

"It's a physical thing." You took a reflective lick of ice cream. We were sitting on one of the iron benches, hell on the back as the decorative grid bit into flesh. "A matter of scale, of the body fitting into the space without gaps. I feel it here." Another lick. "Don't you?"

"Sure," I said, wanting to.

Your head rested against my shoulder. "Why don't we rent a place? Stay put a while. There used to be some nice houses just outside of town."

I sensed a note of false spontaneity. Had this been the idea all along, the moment your finger jabbed the map?

The man with the cart was heading back, this time dragging it by one handle instead of pushing, and the burlap bags were bunched at one end, empty.

"Sure," I said. "I'd love to."

The approach to Apartamentos Vista Hermosa was up a steep unpaved drive. At the foot of the hill we passed a soccer field grazed by two fuzzy horses and next to it stood an adobe house where a woman was scrubbing laundry in outdoor tubs. All around her, sheets and underwear were spread over cactus and shrubbery, bleaching dry. She peered at us as the truck strained up the slope, and answered your wave with a nod.

"More asshole gringos littering the hillside," you chortled.

As the town dropped below, the lake flattened into a disk on the valley floor. You seemed nervous now, grinding the gears and keeping up a steady stream of chatter.

"Travel becomes stupid, the continuum of arrival and departure, always the loop ..." You stopped and let out a low whistle.

We'd twisted around a corner, motor groaning, and now, directly ahead of us, was a line of perfect white adobe houses connected by a long veranda. Behind, the hill continued, brown, with flashes of green, rising to a peak where a wooden cross stood against the intensely blue sky.

You turned to me and grinned, proud as if you'd personally constructed the scene. "You like?"

"I like."

As we drew nearer, bucking over a final pothole, I stared at a man sitting at the end of the veranda. He was tiny and gaunt, with long stringy hair and a goatee — and he stared back with obvious interest, shielding his eyes with a folded magazine.

"I'll be damned!" You took a swipe at the windshield as if it might change the view.

"You know him?"

"Afraid so."

We jerked to a stop and I pushed open the door, but you were already a step ahead. The man on the porch squinted, then broke into a grin.

"Don't tell me — is it the Great Man?"

You kept walking, mounting the steps, one hand dangling the oversize house key.

"How are you doing?" You high-fived without enthusiasm. "Simone, meet Bob. Old Tequila Bob."

Bob waited till I caught up, then lifted a tumbler of clear liquid in salute. "I knew this man back when there were twelve pesos to the dollar." He cackled cheerfully. "He's changed a speck."

"You haven't, Bob, except got more shrunk up."

I was shocked, but Bob took the remark in stride. He laughed, a reedy sound that made his chest sink in. "How many years?"

"Sixteen," you said.

"Really? Time's arrow, man, slips clear through when you're not looking. Shit, I just got here." Bob flashed a set of terrible teeth, then gazed at me. "And this little girl can't be — no sir, I guess not."

I felt my smile tighten. You moved close, pressing to my side.

"And you, Bob?" A hand swept down my spine. "Still queer?"

"As ever. Except now I have to pay for it." He was seized by a fit of coughing.

I took a step backwards; if it was catching, I didn't want it. Bob groped for his drink, spilled half of it, then drained the rest in one snap of the wrist.

"Don't worry, dear," he gasped. "It's only these filthy smokes." Hands trembling, he slid a butt into his mouth and sucked hard. It worked like oxygen and soon he was breathing normally. "Last person up here was a lady poet from Maine. She got sick — amoebas."

I felt you pushing me along the veranda but I hung back, facing Bob. It seemed rude to go when he was still talking.

"Flesh fell off her. All's she could do is drink fucking *té de manzanilla* and chew papaya seeds till one day she toppled over —"

I winced sympathetically.

"You all need to borrow sheets — just ask."

"Who did he think I was?" We stood in front of our doorway; number 4, decorated with a brass knocker in the shape of a fist.

"Don't worry about it." You jammed the key into the lock and yanked on a frayed length of string. There was a faint thunk as the latch inside lifted.

"I think I have a right to know."

The door swung open. We stepped into a small stone courtyard ringed by half a dozen dark rooms. In the middle a jacaranda tree was in full bloom. Mauve petals skimmed the floor as you kicked the door shut.

"You believe it's important?"

I took a breath. "I don't know. This 'we' you refer to —"

Your face soldered shut. "Let's leave now. Don't even unpack. This was an idiotic idea."

I was seized by terror. "That's not what I meant!"

"No, Simone, you're absolutely correct." You swung the bag over your shoulder. "In fact, maybe we should call the whole thing quits. Maybe it's been a mistake from the beginning."

"What are you saying?" I grabbed the wall and felt it flake under my fingers.

You watched this with a pained, distant look, then suddenly seemed to crumple. First you dropped the bag, then sat on top of it.

"What was I ever thinking of?"

Your voice was thick and pitched low .

"A man doesn't deserve such pleasure, such happiness."

I was frantic; what were you talking about?

"And I certainly don't deserve you."

You reached out an arm, still not looking up.

"Come here."

Guarded, I crouched until my face was tucked into your chest. When you began to speak again you set your chin on top of my head.

"Sixteen years ago I came here, right after my first one-man show. I'd sold two pieces to a dentist in Forest Hill and thought I was pretty hot." Your voice was skittery. "Figured all I had to do was paint and it would come: riches, fame, beautiful women. I worked fourteen hours a day, making huge heroic canvases. I thought I was Frank Stella. Hell, better than Stella. All that mattered was the work, then heading downtown at dusk to get drunk. Know what it's like to make a big painting every day? Can you understand that energy, Simone, that *charge*? I didn't care about romance; it was the last thing on my mind."

I felt your heart quicken against my cheek.

"Then one day this girl drives up." You paused. "Carmen."

"Your wife?" I broke away; I needed air. I stared at the damp patch on your shirt, right over your heart.

"I didn't want you to know about this, Simone. I hoped you could just see the place for itself. The ghosts are mine."

You looked distressed, scanning my face for — what? Pain? Signs of indignation? I saw what I could do and, taking a deep breath, rose heroically to the occasion.

"It doesn't matter," I said. "Really."

"It doesn't?"

"No," I continued, thrilled by my courage. "Why should it?"

You looked only briefly suspicious, then, seizing the opportunity, allowed me my lie. "Thank you for that."

I shrugged, bathing in your admiring stare. You couldn't believe your good luck. And what if you were right, that there was no such thing as history; maybe we had both been created this instant, our stories randomly planted in our brains.

"You'll go nuts over this place!" Suddenly we were spinning through each room while you pointed out features; high ceilings, decorated frieze of ceramic tile, carved bed complete with photo of the Virgin of Guadalupe. "And —" you paused dramatically at the last door.

"Ever crap in a jungle?" You kicked it open and we stepped together into a lush garden, a tiny rain forest spilling toward a tilted skylight that let in the achingly intense mountain sun. My eyes dropped to a toilet and the sunken tub coated with mosaic tile.

"Well?"

I realized you were waiting for approval.

"Well?" you insisted, pulling me into your hip.

This, in case you've forgotten, Otto, was the first place we made love in San Patricio, my back pressed against cool tile, the air dense and tropical again, while the faint drip of an imperfectly draining toilet made us think of rain.

The dining room with the cathedral ceiling would be your studio. It was a natural, I agreed. It had the best light and the most open space. I didn't ask, but assumed that it had been your studio before. We would eat in the living room. I helped slide over the heavy table and chairs and swept the floor with a homemade straw broom. There was no dust, only a fine sprinkling of clay.

"You'll need a workplace too," you said when we were done. "How about the second bedroom?"

My own studio. I was delighted. Never mind that it was the smallest room in the house, that it had no ventilation except for the door that led into the courtyard. I was about to live the life of the working artist; hard, compact, and full of possibility.

Later, as we headed out to buy groceries, we passed Bob's door. We had to edge by a table that had been hauled out onto the veranda. A young man with thick black hair, jeans, and a white T-shirt was spreading pieces of pounded tin across its surface. He was stunningly handsome.

"*Buenas tardes*," I said, beating you to it.

He responded with a nod and continued working, forearms flexed, his movements precise and unself-conscious. Then Bob emerged from the house, wearing a stained apron and carrying a trayful of brushes and paint.

"What's all this?" You picked up one of the pieces of tin and flexed it, making a little metallic ping.

"Blame inflation, pal," Bob said. "I'm hustling *folklórico* with Geraldo, to supplement the pension." He wiped his forehead, leaving a streak of pink paint. "These will be wind chimes, our local handicraft." He dropped his tray on the table and grappled for a cigarette.

Geraldo leaned forward with a match while Bob sucked greedily.

I felt you nudge my backside. Was I staring too hard? But he was so young, Otto, his flesh filled his skin and there was nothing in his gesture that was generous, or nervous, or beholden. His face held a detached expression that didn't change despite the intensity of Bob's stare.

"We sell to boutiques in San Miguel," Bob continued. "Tell them it comes from a tiny village, handcrafted by Indians. Hell, after twenty years I feel indigenous. Care to buy one? Real conversation piece back home." He made a dismissive gesture and dropped onto the pigskin chair, pulling his legs up so he was perched in a half-lotus. When he lifted his glasses over his nose he looked suddenly entirely respectable, almost professorial.

"I'd hoped to slip out of the time frame," you said as we tramped downhill, holding the empty shopping bag between us.

I knew what you meant. Bob had blown your cover; he knew who you'd been.

When I turned four years old it was decided that it was high time I learned to read.

"Get a jump on the others," Father said.

What others? I wondered.

He set to work typing index cards on the old Underwood — in English and French, of course — then taped them around the cabin onto the appropriate objects.

Door / *la porte*
Notebook / *le cahier*
Toothbrush / *brosse à dents*
   And even now, as I pour myself a glass of juice, I find myself seizing first the word — then the object.

"Once we recognize an object or situation we immediately give it a name." You pointed to my feet.
   "*Sandal. Toenail.* And it is at that moment we no longer perceive the thing as it is. I want to stop that process and hold off the naming."
   "Yes." I nodded eagerly. I too wanted to see without the scrim of meaning, that dusty net of alphabet — to touch the thing itself.

☼ 9 ☼

TWO BULGING CARDBOARD BOXES contained your essential library, Apollinaire to Zukofsky, and I was making my way through it at a good clip, filling a spiral notebook with jottings. When you disappeared into the cavernous studio for hours on end I would sit in my own "studio" (the word always in quotations) and read. I pretended to myself that this was exactly how I would have it — yet I was aware of every sound that came from the closed room, your (no quotations here) studio. The whistling, the muttered curses, little chirps of delight ... what was I missing? Was that little stutter the sound of scissors cutting through heavy paper? And that abrupt tear — were you ripping apart what you'd made or simply pulling an image from a magazine? At lunch (prepared by me and artfully arranged on clay platters) you seemed aware of my restlessness.

"Keeping busy, Simone?"

"Oh yes."

"Anything to show me?"

"Not yet," I hedged. "Soon."

I didn't want to admit, even to myself, that already I missed our routine of traveling, the jittery stops and starts, the

way we'd pore over the map deciding which tiny town or
hamlet to visit next. And especially the endless hours in the
truck, when I could doze off knowing you would never be
more than a few inches away when I opened my eyes.

You studied me over an *enchilada roja*, then gently slid
the magazine you'd been reading across the table. "Find
thirteen images in here that are the same."

I recognized the shift in your voice to teacher mode
and instantly began flipping through the pages, tilting eagerly
into the challenge.

"And what two images absolutely don't belong
together?" You spoke with your mouth full, unbound by
convention. "Put them side by side and see what happens.
How do they change each other?"

I knew you didn't mean for me to search out any kind
of literal similarity. You meant something different, beyond
"optical." There had to be a conceptual sameness, like thirteen
examples of "openings": buttonholes, doorways, mouths ...

As teacher and student there was something correct,
almost austere in our relationship. You were the one who knew
the answers and it was up to me to seek them out. During these
exchanges it wouldn't have occurred to me to touch you in an
intimate way. Later in the afternoon you might, if you chose,
tiptoe into my room (where I would pretend to be engrossed in
work) and slide your arms around my waist.

I would never enter your studio unannounced.

Another time you ordered me to make a color strip, a
row of matching tonalities. "We're not talking pigment, Simone."

I experimented with the paints, placing them side by
side dozens of ways, adding and subtracting white, changing
hues and intensity, until finally I saw something happening,
how any color, if the tone was adjusted just so, vibrated in
tandem with another. It worked like harmonics, double stops
played skillfully on a violin.

Holding my effort at arm's length you nodded. "That's
it. Now go make a real painting using what you've learned."
Smiling, you added, "You've got a good eye, Simone."

A good eye! Beaming, I hastened back to my room. I was discovering the secret information that would initiate me into the tribe of those-who-know. I was being simultaneously cracked open and filled to the brim.

"How's it going?"

"Pretty good."

"Want me to take a look?"

"Not yet."

"I might be of some use."

Yes. But I couldn't describe the feeling I had, of holding onto something of myself.

You smiled sweetly. "What are you afraid of?"

One day you suggested I place my body in the field outside our house in such a way that I felt not "arranged" but "integral."

"Arranged" was the code word. Artists who didn't bother thinking were mere arrangers of material. They slid forms and colors this way and that until it "looked right."

"Interior decorators," you sneered. "A colony of Bruces."

I earnestly set to finding my way into the exercise, swooping amongst the scrub with Isadora-like gestures, feeling faintly silly, but caught in it, determined.

You stuck your head out the bathroom window. "Stay in your body; don't mimic." Your head disappeared, and when you came back your cheeks were smeared with shaving foam. "And don't fight the landscape; you create more boundaries."

I heard the words and suddenly felt the edges of my body fall away. Again you'd pushed me through the drizzle of self-consciousness, past my own desire to please, to a parched place where I was exhausted — and that was where I began to get it. I stood, one hand anchored to the crumbling adobe wall, sweating, and now I was just a pair of eyes and body parts among these giant cacti and old stone fences. When I moved toward a thing, it got bigger, its surface more detailed — the pores clogged from centuries of wind and dust. When I stepped back, the surface shrank, and the space filled again with sky and earth. When I parsed the air with a weary arm, the air returned quickly to its old shape. Was that it? Was this the lesson, to discover that my presence was temporary, that the world would constantly change, then recover?

"Simone?" you called in a husky voice. "Where did you get to?"

I leaned around the wall and caught sight of you, bare feet hugging the edge of the veranda.

"Simone?"

You were looking in all directions, scanning the hilltop, the washhouse, up and down the pathway. Your brow was creased, your mouth slightly open.

I waited a beat before emerging from the shrubbery.

"Right here."

Relief flashed across your face and your shoulders dropped.

"Well." You stood back and examined me. "Good work, have a beer." You thrust a Dos Equis into my palm.

"When did you learn to do this?" Your hands cupped my ears and you sounded, I thought, a trifle put out.

"I'm making it up as I go along. Everything all right?" I glanced up, trying not to smile. I hadn't told you the whole story about Casey Doyle, my cadet-lover.

"Sure." Still, there was a note of doubt.

Was I being forward, skipping ahead without permission?

"You've done this before." Suspicious, as if you were being made fun of.

"What makes you say that?" I was imagining myself inside your penis, or perhaps, for a few moments, I actually became it, feeling the scratchiness of my tongue as it nimbly flicked across the tip. I was alert to every inflection and quiver, even the brief slackness when you spoke. I responded instantly, quickening or slowing pace, the immaculate accompanist to your growing excitement.

You groaned, leaned back on the chair, legs splayed.

I hesitated a beat, needing to breathe, and suddenly you were pushing my head down.

"Don't stop!" Your back arched. "Don't stop!"

"A remarkable woman, my mother, from very good family." Bob filed at the edge of a piece of tin, creating a spray of metallic dust. "Not exactly Mayflower but the next load. Her people had a huge spread, plains in Nebraska that went clear to ..."

"Yes?" I was gazing down toward the lake at the insect-like boats skimming its surface: *lanchas* taking people back to their villages laden down with market booty. You'd gone downtown, for the first time without me. No fuss had been made, no announcement of intention; you'd simply grabbed your satchel, waved *adios*, and marched down the hill — solo.

"My brother Artie's a shrink in Manhattan. Doctor Artie — confidant to some very heavy types, names you'd know: actors, writers, orchestra conductors ... Then there's the house — I should say 'mansion' — in the Hamptons, jammed every weekend with the 'créme' —" Bob started to cough. He stopped filing, bent double, and shut his eyes, his tiny shoulders heaving. I winced, holding my own breath in sympathy.

You'd said, "These attacks are simply Bob's grammar of presentation, commas that give him time to regroup."

Sure, I thought, except this one looked like a full-stop.

Just as I was going to scoot inside for water, Geraldo stepped from the dark interior of the house wearing only a pair of jeans slung low over his hips. I stared at his navel; perfect, brown, hairless. Bob quit coughing and sat up.

"*¿Que quieres?*" he said.

In response Geraldo slapped the palm of his hand.

Bob muttered a long phrase in his fluent but Yankee-inflected Spanish, then shrugged wistfully.

The boy glared, then disappeared back inside.

"What was that about?"

"My check's late again, poking out the back of some mail sack in Dallas." Bob sighed. "How can I expect this kid, who's never had a fucking thing in his life, to say 'No importa — I don't need pesos, man, only your gorgeous body'?"

Anticipating a cackle, I leaned away — but Bob didn't laugh. Instead, he twisted the piece of tin back and forth till I thought it would snap. I got the idea he was listening: inside the house there were sounds of furniture being dragged over the tile floor. I reached for one of the tin stencils and drew my finger along its sharp edge.

Bob peered at me over his glasses. "What exactly do you need to know?"

I started; was I so transparent? I tried to look puzzled, then faintly offended — then gave in. "Everything! What was he like? What was she like?"

He glanced back into his house; the noises had stopped and he seemed to relax. "I've been here twenty years. I've seen beatnik kids, hippies, artists, writers, dopers — everyone's got a line. Vets who get pie-eyed before noon and murderous at dusk. Bad boys like me. They all say it's 'paradise,' that they'll stay here forever, die in this hard-baked soil — then they clear out inside of three months."

"Because?"

"Because it's so fucking boring. You get sick of greasy tacos and nothing but Charles Bronson movies and Tequila Bob to share the mother tongue. Tired of practicing the same thirty words from the Jiffy phrase book. They start asking, 'How can you stand it here, man?' They quit writing their novel, composing their symphony, searching for God, whatever goddamn thing it is, and spend more and more time at the cantina." Bob paused. "Otto was different."

My belly tightened. "How?"

"He never wondered what to do. He'd paint ten hours every goddamn day before setting foot outside the house — for weeks, months. Hardly saw him until —"

"Yes?"

"One day this girl drives up."

-"Carmen." I'd been waiting for this part, half hoping it wouldn't come, that there was another version of the story.

"With her boyfriend, some tight-ass from New Canaan."

"Boyfriend?" I spoke too eagerly.

"You want the whole story, don't you?" Bob topped off his drink. "Slice me a lime; my hand's a trifle shaky."

I did this.

"Your friend Otto took one look at Carmen in her teensy black sundress and hair down to her waist — and he had to have her."

I swallowed hard.

Bob stuck the lime into a little saucer of salt and drew it around the rim of his glass.

"She hopped up the stairs while that poor bugger of a boyfriend trailed behind hauling suitcases and sweating in his pink polo shirt and chinos. You knew he wasn't going to be in the picture long. Three days later she was meeting Otto behind the gas tanks —" Bob gestured toward the back of the row of houses. "And I was feeding the boyfriend doubles. Bentley? Trying to think of the guy's name ... some car. Chevy?"

"What was she like?" I prompted.

"Classy girl — and didn't have to work at it. The others come down and go native, tearing through the market buying every trinket and embroidered whatsit. But Carmen didn't touch that stuff — didn't need it. She was born with style, bred in her bones."

"Style," I repeated, and stared down at my callused heels wading in a pair of *huaraches*.

Bob cleared his throat and I looked up. You were climbing the path, out of breath, hat pitched off-center. I smiled guiltily and watched your arrival, telling myself you couldn't possibly have heard us.

"Pumping Bob?" You stepped lightly onto the veranda. "I'd rather you didn't."

Unperturbed, Bob pushed the bottle across the table, inviting you to stop. But you were already ducking toward our door. You hadn't so much as glanced at him.

I sprang to follow and Bob was suddenly shouting, "To hell with it. Screw your brains out while you can!"

Then he added in a normal voice. "My own poor pecker's gone AWOL, chased into the hills, scared silly." He raised his glass and looked at me through it, his face startlingly sad.

"Do you consider art a reflection of life?"

I knew this tone, falsely contemplative, and was instantly on guard. "Why look at a reflection," I replied, "if you can look at the thing itself?"

This sounded good to me, so why the excruciating pause? I felt like some poor monk who'd given the wrong answer to the koan. Any moment you'd clobber me over the shoulders and send me packing.

"Or is art therapeutic?" you mused, as if I hadn't uttered a word. "Maybe it's a secret code. Now we're getting somewhere." You drummed the tabletop. "Crack the code ... interpret. Is that it?"

I smiled uneasily.

"Well?" You stared hard.

I tried to look like I was enjoying this.

The silence stretched. Your face wore its teacher guise, impersonal and infinitely patient.

"I guess it's the process of self-expression ..." I ventured.

You grimaced, as if I'd said something awful. Which, of course, I had.

"Art begins," you said in a weary voice, "after we sweep the stables clear of ecstatic moans and shouts."

"So you are an artist, Mr. Guest. You must find Mexico very inspiring."

"Inspiring?"

We were perched at one of the outside tables at Las Flores with Allison Coyne, a retired high school principal from Bolinas.

"In what sense?" you said, one finger skimming the rim of your coffee cup.

"The gorgeous colors, the mountain light, the depth of suffering in these marvelous Indian faces ..."

I struggled not to laugh, at the same time hoping you wouldn't be too hard on her. She had confided to us earlier that she was in remission from bone cancer.

"My painting is the same everywhere," you said. "Place has nothing to do with it."

"Then you must be an abstractionist, Mr. Guest."

"Do you know what that means?"

"Certainly." She flashed a smile. "That there's nothing to look at that says anything."

You were delighted. "A fine definition, best I've ever heard!"

We stopped for ice cream, part of the daily ritual. But instead of ordering, you hesitated in the doorway and stared back into the square.

"What?" I followed your gaze but saw nothing unusual; only some uniformed schoolchildren racing full-tilt toward home.

"We came here after leaving the clinic." Your voice was low and I had to strain to hear. "The doc, some old coot named Valenzuela, said, '*Señora, esta embarazada,*' then shook our hands and congratulated us."

Your hip bounced off the stone wall. Your hand, holding a cigarette, was trembling.

You clenched the little square packet in your teeth and ripped it open. You did this, as always, twice — while I lay naked on the sheet.

Double protection. Inner and outerwear.

"Can't be too careful," you said.

"No, sir," I agreed, matching emphasis.

☀ 10 ☀

"BRING THOSE hands over here!"

Mother's voice was unaccustomedly firm. She stood at the kitchen counter unscrewing the lid from the blue jar of Nivea.

I half enjoyed this ritual, rolling back the sleeves of my flannel nightgown and offering my hands while she laid down an impasto of cold cream over chapped winter skin. Outside the cabin a bitter wind tore through the trees, then whistled through the chinks of roof board, while inside, a fire blazed, and the old crank gramophone (relic from an auction) scratched its way through an Ezio Pinza 78.

She slathered Nivea a quarter-inch thick over each hand, then reached up and dolloped my elbows.

Next came the white cotton gloves, freshly laundered each day, with seams that ran down each finger and across the back, like veins.

She opened the first glove and drew it over my hand, tugging sharply over the wrist.

"Next."

The procedure was repeated.

"You'll thank me one day when you have lovely soft

skin." She grazed her own knuckles against my cheek and I marveled at their smoothness.

"All today's artist needs is a pair of sharp scissors and a stick of Elmer's Glue," you declared. "Make new images from the old; it's an ecological necessity." Your scissors attacked a copy of *Hola* magazine, snipping through the tanned torso of Julio Iglesias.

We sat on the crumbling stucco wall above the house sipping margaritas and watching the sunset pour over the lake.

"It's a mistake for an artist to marry," you said. "Duchamp was right; the family forces you to abandon your real ideas."

I nodded earnest agreement. I certainly had no interest in what you called the "three Bs": babies, barbecues, and bungalows.

"You look pretty in this light." I felt your hand drape over my shoulder then slip toward my breast. I leaned in to accommodate.

"You'll be incredible when you're older. I envy the guy who hooks up with you in ten years." The hand snuck under my blouse. Right in broad daylight. Not that anyone much came up our hill: Jehovah's Witnesses, the man who sold firewood, the gas truck every two weeks. We were huddled just above the row of houses where they petered into ugly slabs of concrete with iron rods poking out the sides. Dislodged roof tiles had fallen, littering the ground with chunks of red clay. On top of each roof were the water tanks, concrete lozenges with seams running lengthwise, balanced on platforms. This was your favorite viewpoint, you claimed. Because from here we could see how the buildings worked.

"I could do this all night," you sighed, looking up from where you'd buried your face between my breasts.

By now my blouse was unbuttoned and your tongue swam over my flesh, the wetness drying instantly in the crisp evening air.

"This isn't right, you know."

"It isn't?" I smiled. I'd heard this before.

"I was your teacher, in a position of authority."

I hesitated only a second. "Who cares?"

"The thing is," you said, caressing my nipples lightly with your fingertips, "it feels too sweet to stop."

My own hand, silky after years of being anointed with Nivea and the white glove, reached inside your underwear.

I caught sight of your back first; the rest of you was hidden by the pillar in front of Las Flores. I loved meeting you by chance downtown. We would act out the delight of reunion as if we hadn't seen each other for days. I would watch your expression change from a reflective frown to a grin of recognition. I saw you as others might; an older man greeting his pink-cheeked girlfriend, and how you would touch my hair, laughing, as if you could hardly believe your good fortune.

You were not alone.

I'd already crossed the plaza, smiling broadly in anticipation, but began to slow down as I watched you lean over the table in that earnest way I knew well, index finger probing the place mat. I inched forward, changing angle, so I could see who you were speaking to.

She was Mexican, dressed in a topaz-colored cardigan embedded with dozens of tiny pearls. Shoulder-length hair swept behind a pair of ornate silver earrings, and, like you, she was smoking.

I slowed down to a creep.

"Simone!"

I pretended not to hear.

"Simone!"

I made a show of hesitation, even looked toward the

sky as if trying to locate the direction of the call. I assumed a puzzled expression.

"Over here," you cried.

Your friend waved long, red-painted fingernails.

I waved back, open-mouthed, a parody of delighted recognition.

"This is Adela."

The woman rose and gently took my hand. I thought she looked amused: had she seen through my little mime show?

I pumped too vigorously and watched her flinch.

"Adela runs a private school," you said as she removed her hand, discreetly flexing it.

"A very small one," she added. Her English was accented just enough to be charming. I guessed her to be about your age. Her hair, beginning to gray, was tucked into a ponytail. A deep line bisected her forehead. She looked wise and interesting.

You hooked a chair from a neighboring table and dragged it over.

"Won't you join us?"

Your tone, I thought, seemed too formal. But I sat down, pressing my hands between my knees, then sliding them out when I decided the pose was childish.

"I have asked Otto to teach an art class to my boys and girls," Adela said.

Ot-to: she spoke your name with two distinct syllables.

"And what did he say?"

"Like a real Mexican he tells me, 'Why not?' "

I gazed at the empty cups with their milky frill. You two had been here a while. How had you met? Did she invite herself to your table, or did you meet someplace else, perhaps in the cool hallway of the Bellas Artes, and end up here. I studied your face for a sign, and saw nothing but a relaxed smile.

Beyond you, standing under the shade of the *portales*, was the man who sold *pan integral*. He was slipping his delicious whole-wheat rolls into a paper bag for a woman who seemed to be grumbling about the price. We had been trying to figure out a pattern in his selling methods. Was it Tuesday and Thursday evenings? Then he'd turn up on a hot Saturday afternoon with his straw basket. We decided that he baked when he felt like it, and sold when he was in the mood. "To look for a pattern," you explained, "is to impose our needs over his."

Suddenly Adela rose to her feet. "I must go back to my office. I am so pleased to meet you, Simone." She reached across the table and gave me a light *beso* on each cheek, then, resting her fingertips on your shoulder, performed the same gesture.

You rose to reciprocate, but she was already racing across the plaza, her high heels expertly clipping against stone.

I said, with what was intended to be offhand curiosity, "Does she have family here?"

"If you mean, is she married, the answer is I don't know." You tilted your chair back precariously. "That good enough for you?"

I worked on Utopia with Dad for years. We laid out our village bit by bit on the picnic table in the mudroom; this was my childhood's version of a dollhouse with its miniature structures and furniture, tiny woven rugs and clay dishes. We built scaled-down aqueducts and tepees, longhouses and Hopi Indian domes, even pyramids scrupulously copied from encyclopedia drawings.

"A modern Utopia," Father said, dipping his brush and applying varnish to the roof of the Haida longhouse, "appropriates visions from all cultures. How are you doing with that rocker?"

"Not bad." I was sanding a diminutive eighteenth-century Upper Canadian rocking chair, its no-nonsense frame held together with tiny screws and finishing nails.

"What makes this truly Utopian," his brush poised mid-air, "is the fact that there are no people around to mess it up."

Whenever Father said this I felt the same faint dampness in the air, a whiff of suffocation that I hadn't yet put a name to.

"The pyramid will be the consultation chamber for elders," he added.

"For Pete's sake." Mother glanced at our efforts as she pushed against the outer door. "Those things were tombs."

She was carrying her string bag, which held a Thermos of tea and a Dickens novel. This meant she was headed into the woods for the rest of the afternoon.

"What on earth does she do out there?" Father stared through the streaked window. There was no use in asking her, he knew. Mother's response to direct questions was an enigmatic smile — and silence. She would return, hours later, calves scratched and muddy, offering no explanation.

The sun shifted as we continued our efforts. One of my specialties was inventing miniature labor-saving devices for our colony; intricate systems of strings and matchsticks, pulleys and levers, that would perform the tedious tasks that no proper Utopian would be bothered with. I built a chute leading from the scaled-down Louis Quinze table in the Mayan eating hut to the washing sink. The dishes would shoot right into the soapy water with one crank of the tiny lever.

"You have entirely the wrong attitude about manual labor," Father remarked. "Washing dishes, if performed with attention and respect, is no less a task than composing the finale of a sonata."

I snickered. "Let's see you try it then."

He'd never cleaned a dish in his life.

"What does she do out there?" He brushed sawdust off his trousers and gazed out the window. I got the idea he hadn't stopped thinking about her for a minute.

When she did return, hours later, he jumped to his feet.

"Nice walk? Get as far as the marsh?"

He never gave up hope she'd tell him. Instead, she smiled and deposited a Thermos full of wild strawberries on the kitchen counter.

I could hear his mind buzzing. Berries? Must be near the town line. Or the bat cave.

"Simone?" She dunked her hands into a bucket of water and scrubbed energetically. "Why don't we make these into a pie?"

Whenever Father left the cabin, for whatever reason, there would be a full report on his return. In a hearty voice he'd proclaim, "Hell of a fine day, girls. The birds are in top form — saw the heron gliding toward the swamp, with a nice pickerel pinched in his beak. The dock will need new footings and a coat of paint. Judy? You'll be glad to know that mountain ash you planted made it through the winter. Jude? I say that mountain ash you planted ..."

I lay on my back on your studio cot and laughed, then quickly clapped a hand over my mouth. This, I decided, was the dopiest moment in our relationship. We'd started out with a lesson in "negative space as perceived in the Renaissance" — the fat book of Leonardo was still open on your table — when suddenly, after framing a corner of the reproduction with your hands, you'd thwacked the page.

"Want to know what I'm really thinking about?"

"The future of official bilingualism?"

That's when you grabbed me. It was always a turn-on, these sudden transitions from teacher to lover.

"Be right back." Clinging to your trousers you headed for the bathroom.

To pee? Wash up? I shucked what remained of my own clothes, lay down on the cot, and waited. The ceiling in your studio pitched to a cathedral point. A net of cobwebs reached from side to side, flecked red with clay dust.

Faucets were turned on and off; the toilet flushed. Any minute now.

I readied myself, one leg sloped sideways, an arm looped over my head.

An odd moment to find oneself alone; too much time to think. Should I have brushed my teeth? My tongue darted in search of lettuce shreds, stray crumbs. And what about — down there? I grabbed a corner of the sheet and wiped vigorously.

Your footsteps trotted across the tile floor, but then, instead of growing louder and firmer, they became fainter. I heard a door creak open. Straining, now propped on one elbow, I listened to the sigh of mattress. You'd gone into our bedroom, which was where I was supposed to be, waiting.

That's when I started to giggle, picturing you lying naked, half-erect, wondering where the hell I was.

Seconds ground by as I lay, hand pressed to my mouth, until at last your voice, sounding slightly peeved, called out, "Simone, where are you?"

"In here."

A pause while you digested this, neither of us moving a muscle, our bodies divided by open courtyard and foot-thick clay walls.

"Well get yourself in here."

When I arrived at the bedroom door I hardly dared look at you. The situation seemed freighted with a symbolism I wasn't anxious to pursue.

We made love quickly, as if laughter, once embarked on, might never leave us.

☀ 11 ☀

"BRANCUSI, WHO WAS no hick, said there's a right physical size for every idea. Let's consider this." Your eyes narrowed as you gazed around the courtyard, its bumpy stone floor, the immense potted plants that needed watering. "What is the right size for the idea of 'small'?"

Then you disappeared into your studio, leaving me charged up, head buzzing.

Small.

No, the "idea of small" — the collision between expectation and event, between what is anticipated and what is encountered.

The girl on the footbridge was no more than fourteen. She smiled shyly as I passed and I nodded back, then glanced under her arm. My smile froze. She was carrying a tiny gray coffin wrapped in plastic, no more than a foot and a half long. The price sticker dangled on a cardboard tag.

The idea of small.

You liked to get out on your own. We were separate people, not like those gringo couples stepping off the bus for day trips, clad in twin safari jackets and Reeboks, and hefting sensible canvas bags.

You taught twice a week at Adela's school, from one to one forty-five in the afternoon. The first time you were back by two, full of funny descriptions, how the kids had trooped into the room carrying little paper cups full of stubby crayons, singing, "*¡Buenas tardes señor Guest!*"

"Come and see for yourself."

"I'd like to."

Except the next time you didn't ask. In fact you didn't get home till dark, and then no explanation was offered. Instead you poured yourself a drink and took it to the veranda.

"I'm off." You ripped a traveler's check from the stash hidden at the back of the fridge.

I hovered by the door. "Off to where?"

I should have known better. When you didn't answer, I lingered on the steps and watched you clump down the hill on foot.

"Where is the Great Man headed?" Bob squinted under his green sun visor.

"I have no idea," I snapped. "We don't exchange itineraries."

Then I had to pretend to myself and Bob that I wasn't waiting. But that's exactly what I was doing.

Only when I heard your whistle approach would my brain and heart engage. Only when you were near did every pore in my skin yawn open, my cells bristle in readiness.

"Thing is," Bob announced without prompting, "Otto doesn't really like women, though he sure as hell needs them. On the other hand, I don't need them, which allows me to like them."

There was no clear sightline down the dirt road as it sank, twisting and turning, to the highway below. Clumps of cacti clung to the slope, leaves blossoming like prickly spatulas, surfaces poised to catch any stray raindrop. Others, at a distance, looked like the bushes back home, until, moving closer, thick fingers grew instead of paper-thin leaves. Every time a bus passed, grinding around the curve, overloaded with passengers and market loot, a plume of grisly diesel smoke rose and dispersed into the air.

A chameleon sunned with endless patience on the lip of our roof. Hummingbirds whirred, their beating wings invisible as they hovered over Bob's bright red feeder.

Waiting.

There was so much of that.

Waiting while you worked in your studio.

Waiting to see what mood you'd be in when you finally flung open the door. Adventure, anyone? Want to go to that village where they make blue pottery?

Do I?

How about an overnighter to the abandoned mission house?

Sure.

The birthplace of some revolutionary leader, or take a *lancha* across the lake and see the house where André Breton was reputed to have stayed.

I needed you to breathe life into me. I'd lost the knack of cranking myself up.

You came home smelling of stables. I breathed deeply but spoke not a word. Perhaps as a reward for my discretion, you said, "I met a wonderful German woman. She drove me to her hacienda."

"Oh?" My stomach tightened.

"A perfectly intact turn-of-the-century spread. Her uncle built it. Herr Wolfgang. Massive stables, outbuildings, orchards ..." You gestured enthusiastically, your face flushed. "And we drank iced coffee under a gnarled apple tree." You danced on tiptoes. Your shirt was imperfectly tucked in. I found myself examining the fabric for grass stains.

I thought about the hours I'd spent on the hill, glancing every ten minutes down the road, waiting.

"I'm glad someone had an interesting day."

Your hands dropped. "What's wrong with you?"

I shrugged miserably, hating myself.

"It happens," you said in a formal, cold voice, "that Elsa Gluck is seventy-three years old."

You marched into your studio and slammed the door.

"You don't understand the phases of the moon yet? Pass me that piece of paper."

Father would launch into a diagram at the drop of a hat. He loved to explain as his hand moved over the page. Anything. Phases of the moon, sewage systems in ancient Rome, the formation of tropical hurricanes. Out came the chunky HB pencil, hand-whittled, and the back of an envelope scrunched against his knee.

"There, isn't that clearer?" He smoothed his effort, smiling with secret pleasure.

When I got older I used to sigh "Here goes" when the pencil came out. But the truth was, I liked hovering over his shoulder as he made his careful renderings and painstaking captions. It was the soft scrape of pencil lead over paper I listened to, and the way his voice would drop when he knew he had my attention.

Item: a long black hair snagged in your buttonhole.

So what? Lots of girls at the school wore their hair loose to the waist. Little girls. I placed the hair against a sheet of dark paper and held it up to the light. I saw what I knew I'd see, what I'd dreaded — the streak of gray at its root.

Adela probably left hairs like this everywhere, clogging up sinks, and floating in bowls of soup.

I took a perverse pleasure in chronicling minutely the details of your lovemaking; your hand as it dove inside her blouse, her amused look, a heel pushing against the office door for privacy, those red-lacquered fingernails gliding into your pants. When I closed my eyes I even felt how it would be inside her mouth, tasting faintly of cilantro and cigarettes, how your lips and tongue would swell in that dark, wet place. I would become both you and her, in turn, then simultaneously. A hermaphrodite, I was your hard body sinking into hers, then the soft fleshy other tugging with my thighs.

Item: you lit the fire, kneeling on the tile floor, reaching with a wooden match. My eye shot to the box, attracted by its unfamiliar logo.

"Restaurante Don Vasco?" I read aloud. "You always swore you'd never set foot in the place."

The D.V. was a notorious clip joint run by the ex-police-chief's daughter.

You just smiled. "Don't miss much, do you, Simone?"

Item: "What's this?" I ran my hand down your sleeve. The white shirt had developed a mauve stain the size of a hundred-peso coin. We'd had rain that afternoon, an unexpected dousing that had been gulped by the parched ground and left not a trace, except your damp hair and this swatch of color.

You yanked the material around, cursing. "My one decent shirt. Will it come out?"

Purple.

Adela's shawl, of course. She always wore it slung over her shoulders, the spidery ends trailing down her back.

"Give it to me," I said, seizing the garment. "I might be able to do something."

I wanted the chance to examine it up close, match dyes and fibres.

I mapped out your days in my mind, penciling in what I thought you might be doing, then etching it permanently when (and if) I found out for sure. There were huge gaps, like those early explorers' maps full of wild guesses and unarticulated blobs. At night I ransacked your pockets for scraps of paper, matchboxes, any item I couldn't readily explain. A bank receipt, a candy wrapped in lint. You never ate candy.

All my gestures began to misfire. I was trying too hard.

I thought I was doing you a favor when I taped the Polaroids of Kip, your son, to the fridge door.

"Why did you do this?" Already you were peeling them off.

"I thought —"

"If I wanted them there I would have taped them up myself."

"I was just trying —"

"I know." Then, more kindly, you added, "I needn't be reminded what a colossal fuck-up I am every time I reach for a beer."

The problem, of course, was boredom. This was the chilling fall into tedium Bob had spoken of, when piece by piece paradise disintegrates into long, formless days, and pricks of anxiety swell into obsession. I wouldn't have minded if you too were growing restless. But you weren't. On the contrary, you'd never been more content, working long hours in your studio, taking off on little journeys by yourself, and teaching. You'd stretch out your arms, fingers interlocked, and wait until the knuckles snapped. This would be followed by a long sigh.

"It's all right here, isn't it, Simone?"

"My sister's coming." Mother slipped the embossed greeting card back into the pink envelope. Her voice was tense yet eager.

"Aunt Amy?" I chirped. "When?"

"Tomorrow evening, by the looks of it."

"Batten down the hatches." Father heaved himself out of the chair and brushed off his shirt. Litter clung to his clothes and surrounded him on all sides; pencil shavings, a string of used dental floss, books and magazines held open by coffee mugs, and a ceramic bowl overflowing with peanut shells. "I better go downtown for a bottle of rye. Your Amy likes to tuck in soon as her feet touch ground."

As exciting as Aunt Amy's actual arrival was the immediate disruption in our routine; a sense of bustle descended — entirely welcome from my point of view. Father bumped down the hill in the car to pick up a bottle of Canadian Club from the LCBO while Mother began to hum and flip open the *Harrowsmith Cookbook* — cake and pastry section. I grabbed a broom and began to sweep energetically. Aunt Amy was used to broadloom and central vac. She had a "Polish lady" who came once a week to do her house. Mother's humming burst into a chorus from *Oklahoma!* as she beat eggs into the mixing bowl.

"Oh what a beautiful mor-ning —"

"I remember," she interrupted herself as flour sifted into the mound of butter and eggs, "the time your aunt and I hitchhiked to Saskatoon to see Art Pepper. We were real jazz nuts."

"You were?"

First I'd heard.

"We even went backstage and got our picture taken with Mr. Pepper, then ..." She smiled, sank the spoon into the batter, and leaned on it.

"Then?"

"His suit was so smooth and shiny, like abalone shell. I suppose I must have the snapshot somewhere."

"And here is something for our Simone." Aunt Amy passed over a small rectangular package, wrapped professionally in foil.

I giggled self-consciously and tore apart the wrapping.

Inside was an elegant pale green container, which snapped open with the help of Aunt Amy's fingernails.

"Ooooh," we crooned conspiratorially.

Inside was a palette of eye shadow, each color in its separate compartment, the surfaces immaculately ridged, like an aerial view of the fields midsummer. I picked up the tiny hygienic Q-tip and gave a tentative dab.

"What the hell is she going to do with this stuff out here?" Father snorted.

"She won't always be 'out here,'" Aunt Amy said.

Father's mouth clamped shut and he assumed the besieged look that would remain in place until Aunt Amy hiked her bags back to Regina.

Mother always got some obscure kitchen device, like an olive pitter, or lemon zester, or frilly bits of paper to decorate a crown roast. These would be placed, after appropriate expressions of delight, into a drawer where they would gather dust. Father always got a book. Aunt Amy knew that he liked to read and had her own ideas what he should be interested in.

"Is this what you call 'historical fiction'?" Warily he flipped the book over and examined the author photograph: a buxom woman in a crushed Irish hat held a walking stick. In the background was Stonehenge.

Aunt Amy was bordering on stout and always wore print dresses that were a fraction too tight. Mother called her an "optimistic dresser," meaning that she was full of certainty that one day her diet attempts would kick in and the garment would miraculously drape over her hips with cloth to spare. She wore a girdle. I knew this because the lines were visible when she crossed her legs, or when she stood on the porch at dusk sipping a cocktail and the breeze flattened her dress against her thighs and belly.

"Glorious!" she would exclaim as the sun sloped below the horizon leaving a sky shot with orange. "Almost as good as the prairie."

I had the idea that she was carefully constructed from the inside out, unlike my mother, who seemed to require minimal maintenance.

Aunt Amy made no effort to adapt to country life. She wore three-inch heels and pantyhose, even when we were hiking through the woods. The thing was, she could keep up perfectly well in her city clothes and threaded nimbly between strands of barbed wire without snagging anything. At night she would rinse out her hose, bra, and panties, and sling them over a kitchen chair in front of the stove to dry. This embarrassed me — the idea that my father would brush by these undergarments, which were so lacy and unabashedly feminine. Mother, when she bothered to wear a bra at all (strictly for town trips), preferred the sturdy cross-your-heart model where form and function were perfectly wedded.

Aunt Amy always brought an oversize bag of hard candies that she'd picked up at the Regina airport because she couldn't stand the dry air in the plane. Each visit was marked by a particular smell and flavor; one year it was mint, another year English toffee, and the year of the eye shadow was, I am certain, butter rum.

"Now what?" Aunt Amy sat back after morning coffee. She never ate breakfast. "Can't stay cooped up here all day, can we? Where are you girls going to take me?"

I never felt "cooped up" until Aunt Amy pointed it out. Couldn't we stare for hours at the clear, uncluttered horizon?

"What about the bird sanctuary in Markton, then over to the mill for lunch?" Mother was wearing her wraparound skirt and a crisp paisley blouse. She was slightly flushed and her movements had become vigorous, as if the cabin were too confining.

"Right-o." Amy picked up her stiff leather handbag, a pair of dark glasses, and we set off, crying a chorus of "See you later" to Father, who stood on the porch watching forlornly as we drove down the hill.

"What's he saying?" Aunt Amy craned around in her seat.

"Not to order shellfish or anything with cream in it," Mother answered, without a glance back.

"You know, Jude," Aunt Amy said on her last night. "It's very pretty here but I don't know how you get through the winters." She shivered. "Talk about claustrophobia."

"Claustro-phobia?" I said. "What's that?" My eyelids were pasted with slate gray eye shadow.

"It means —" Mother perched on the edge of the dining table and crossed her legs. "A feeling of being trapped, closed in, suffocated."

Father opened his mouth as if to say something, then turned the gesture into a cough.

After Amy left, there was what Father called "residual effect" for several days. Mother would be flushed and bad-tempered, particularly with him. When he began to read aloud from the *Guardian* she put down her own book and snapped,"For Heaven's sake!"

"What?" He sounded hurt.

"Just listen to yourself!"

He looked at me, shrugging, hoping to enlist my sympathy. But I too was edgy. Claustrophobia? Didn't we have the best view in the country? Couldn't we see clear over the tops of three towns on a good day? Wasn't it the poor suckers trapped in cities that felt closed in? Those fools who peered from sealed office towers into tiny chinks of sky and called it breathing?

"He figured if he kept her away from the world she would forget about it," I said wisely.

You gave me a curious smile.

"He thought he could create a 'safe house' where we would be immune to the influences of modern life."

"Indeed." Your hand caressed my shoulders. You liked hearing me talk about my family.

"I wonder if he ever asked her," I went on.

"Asked her what?"

"If this was the way she wanted to live."

"What do you think?"

"That he wouldn't dare. What if she said no? It's like asking someone if he loves you — better not ask if you're not damn sure of the answer."

You nodded and pulled a shred of tobacco from between your teeth.

I watched Mother grab a handful of cutlery from the drainer, then instead of arranging the pieces in their proper compartments, she stood motionless, fist in the air, smiling.

"Your mother," Father observed, "is having a thought, possibly an illumination —"

The slightly pleased look dropped from her face. Cutlery poured into the open drawer every which way.

"That should do it." I set the neatly sectioned grapefruit on the table before you. A drizzle of sugar had already begun to dissolve. Had there been a cherry I would certainly have popped one in the middle.

You leaned in and pried loose a section. I was pleased to watch it slide effortlessly onto your spoon.

You looked up, eyes narrowed.

"You've already cut it."

"Of course."

"Every section — even around the middle."

I nodded.

"Simone," you said wearily, "I can carve my own grapefruit."

My drawings were starting to look like yours. Gone was the cautious thready line of the old days. I'd ditched the Rapidograph pen that you'd condemned as being "prissy," and switched to a fat felt-tip marker.

"Make lines on the page without defining a shape," you challenged.

I thought you sounded distracted, even a little sad.

I drew lines but shape snuck in like water over a sandbar.

"It can't be done!" I said at last. "You make a line, shape happens on its own."

"Is it possible to love without confining the loved one?" you said.

You composed a still life by reaching into your pocket, pulling out a wrinkled packet of Delicados, and tossing it onto the table. Then, moving about the room, you snatched a magazine, fork, a chunk of cheese, a handful of dry spaghetti and tossed them carelessly onto the table.

"*Nature morte.* Let's see what you can do."

I was sure now I detected a note of impatience.

Later you wandered over to my sketchboard and swept a hand over one section of the paper.

"This bit's nice." A finger stabbed at a point in the upper quadrant. "Here you lose it."

You could read my line with absolute clarity, pinning down the instant where I lost contact, where I'd hoped to get away with something.

☀ 12 ☀

"YOO-HOO, LOVEBIRDS!" Bob poked his head in our doorway. He was clad in a red bandanna and a pair of baggy shorts held up with a sash. "Come on over, pronto — I got a ton of fuckin' chicken and no mouths to feed." He waved a boning knife. "Geraldo, the Divine, has split."

"For good?" you said.

"*Quien sabe*, man. The kid grabbed his undies and comic books and flew back to Mama."

Bob's apartment had the same clay floor as ours, grouted with thick coils of mortar. The furniture was a mix of Mexican Colonial (heavy dark wood and rigid chair backs) and bits of Americana by way of the Sally Ann. There was a couch, green upholstery with threadbare arms, circa 1965, and a tiny black-and-white TV set. On top of the TV was a silver-framed photograph of an elderly couple. They stood side by side, unsmiling, in front of a New England-style clapboard house.

"Your folks?" I said.

"Ma and Pa Kettle."

They were far from that. Bob's father wore khaki pants held up with suspenders, a pinstriped shirt, and a battered straw hat. He was frowning through a pair of rimless glasses. Clenched under one arm was a rolled-up copy of *New Yorker* magazine. His wife, perhaps a dozen years younger, wore her hair pulled back in a no-nonsense style so that her face seemed to jut toward the picture-taker. Bob looked just like her; same cheekbones, same wiry build. She seemed, I thought, faintly annoyed.

"Back here, dear."

The kitchen was at the rear of the apartment, through the courtyard. His stove was older and bigger than ours, with a warming oven and a rusty pipe that poked through the ceiling. Tacked to the wall over the counter was a faded travel poster from Switzerland, showing a picture-perfect village nestled in the Alps.

Bob pointed at the poster with the tip of his knife. "My prep school: L'Académie Renaud. Bunch of rich American brats chasing the local girls. But I fell in love with the housemaster — Ernst from Bern."

His knife left a spot of grease in the corner of the picture.

Every kitchen device Bob owned was spread over the tiled counter; ancient rusty spatulas, hand-carved wooden spoons, a wire whisk, and a stained mortar and pestle. Vegetables tumbled out of web bags while a hefty chicken carcass rolled in the sink, a stream of water running over it.

"Were you expecting an army?" I said.

"That's just it, dear, I was. Mama and Papa and three nasty sisters. It's the kid's *cumpleaños* — nineteen years old today. Here, have a drink." Bob passed me a bottle and two spotty tumblers, which I discreetly rubbed on my sleeve.

We perched on the edge of the table as Bob worked. He chopped and hacked, taking frequent swallows of tequila, and talked non-stop.

"I told the little fucker I loved him. First mistake. I said, 'Don't go away to school, stay here, help me with the wind chimes.' I groveled, I pleaded, bribed, and finally threatened."

"And?" Bob's misery made me feel oddly elated.

He tossed a section of chicken into the pan, then turned around. "Know what the fucker said?"

"What?"

"'You'll never own a man like me if you live a thousand years.'"

I winced at the expression on his face, and the voice pitched too high. Then I looked your way. You were staring at Bob intently, leaning forward and nodding — but not, to my relief, laughing.

"Yes!" you shouted suddenly. "The thing you got to understand, Bob, the words we must all tattoo on our chests are —" and here you began to draw oversize letters in the air and recite: "*EL...DUEÑO...DE...NADA.*"

Sure, I remembered. It was the slogan painted over the grille of a rickety Chevy pickup we'd spied parked in town the day before. The Owner of Nothing.

"It's a state to aspire to," you continued, moving your face close to Bob's. "The simplicity of freedom."

Unimpressed, Bob nibbled on a raw onion, then breathed into your face. "Maybe I don't want simple." Then he set his glasses onto the end of his nose and peered down at a neatly typed list. "Maybe I think you're full of shit."

I sucked in hard, and fixed my attention on the list: chicken with lime, sautéed *calabazas*, grilled potatoes, rice, and ... D.O.D.

"What's that?" I said, pointing to the last item.

"Dessert of the Day," Bob said, scrutinizing with me. "It was supposed to be a cake."

Suddenly you slipped off the table. You towered over Bob and when he edged toward the stove you followed, hovering by his shoulder.

"It's a bitch, isn't it? Let yourself tilt into another person and you end up pulling down both of you. Never underestimate the forces of gravity, Bob."

You slung an arm over his shoulder while your free hand picked at the chopped vegetables and popped them into your mouth. I nearly said something; they hadn't been soaked in iodine-treated water. They hadn't even been peeled.

"Look at her!" You pointed in my direction. "She doesn't know a thing about this, about bone-crushing pain." Your hand dropped. "What could such a blessed state be like?"

I felt my face blaze red, and it wasn't the tequila. My fingernails dug into the tabletop. You kept staring, your face full of undisguised wonder.

Later I grabbed a cold tortilla, wrapped it around a piece of half-cooked chicken, and took it out to the veranda. The meal had never materialized. Back inside Bob's apartment a tinny radio blared mariachi tunes and you two were lurching around, imitating ballroom dancers.

But hadn't you first tugged my arm, saying with elaborate courtesy, "May I have the honor?"

And hadn't I shrugged you off, annoyed by your good spirits, which seemed off-pitch and aggressive?

"Ask him," I said, meaning Bob. "Your fellow sufferer."

"What's that noise?"

"Who cares?" Mother yawned and turned over.

For the third time I heard Father slide off the bed and huff around the cabin, testing windows, doorways, and the stove. He lifted a heavy iron burner and let it drop with a godawful clatter. Rodent? Bird trapped in the chimney?

"You may laugh," I heard him say when he settled back into bed. "It could be a clogged propane line, the chimney not venting. We'll be found tomorrow, gassed and fried to a crisp."

I didn't intend to follow you. I crossed the pebbled street at the corner of Garcia and 20 de Noviembre aiming for the hardware store. My fingers slipped between the pages of the pocket dictionary: *ratonera*.

Mousetrap. I hoped he wouldn't think we had *rats*.

Suddenly, framed in the doorway I was intending to enter, I saw you folding a wad of peso bills into your pocket. Without thinking, I darted into another doorway where I stood, hidden.

I'd been caught off guard, I told myself. The minutes ground by: you lit a cigarette, adjusted your hat, and exhaled while other customers squeezed by, muttering "*Con permiso*." You seemed to be weighing options, deciding where to go next. Squinting into the sun you stared directly at me, and I quickly began to lift a hand in salute.

Then I understood you hadn't seen me, and stepped back into the shadows, flattening myself against the wall. I could see behind you into the dark interior of the hardware store. Behind the counter hung a display of gleaming copper keys. And dangling from a string attached to the ceiling was a giant cardboard key twisting in the breeze, slung so low the proprietor had to keep ducking.

At last, setting a pair of sunglasses on your nose, you began to walk — not east, as I'd anticipated (toward the central plaza), but south, downhill. You headed along Independencia and I followed, a steady twenty yards behind. The walls of the buildings were studded with windows, red frames painted directly on the stucco, and protected by decorative iron grids. Most didn't have glass panes. We jogged down, past a tiny craft store I'd never noticed. A young girl was just shutting the door, but not before I'd glimpsed Bob's wind chimes hanging from the ceiling inside. Next intersection, I told myself, I'll call out your name as if I'd just spied you. But I didn't. Instead I continued to follow as you crossed a rickety bridge that spanned the dried-up creek bed and tramped toward a part of town I'd never been to. You'd pointed this way once, saying, "Cantina land, strictly for the menfolk."

The moment for hailing was long past. Each time I opened my mouth to call your name, something stopped me. I told myself it was instructive to watch you this way, scaled human size, a man like any other walking down the road. Your hips swung gently with the slope and I imagined that your left knee, the one you'd wrecked in high school soccer, was beginning to lock. We'd long left the center of town and were passing joints with names like El Gato Negro and La Oficina with saloon-style doors, canned music, and the stench of stale booze. I became increasingly uneasy. The streets petered out from cobblestone to dirt, pitted and rutted from the rainy season. The buildings were unpainted adobe and there wasn't a scrap of greenery in sight. No maids sloshed pails of washwater into the street, no uniformed children heaved book bags. Except for the music there was a curious silence. Men slouched outside the bars, legs sprawled, chin resting on chest, sleeping, or dead drunk, or plain dead. They wore the campesino uniform of jeans, plaid shirt, and ancient straw hat. I kept my eyes firmly fixed on your shoulders. You continued the trek downhill, twisting around corners, and the buildings grew more insubstantial each block, now tacked together with sheets of corrugated tin. And where were the women? I glanced backwards. Could I even find my way to the center? There was no sign of the beckoning church spire, or the treetops of the plaza. I picked up my pace; you were my protection. Then an unpleasant thought crossed my mind: what if you knew I was tailing you? Perhaps you'd caught a glimpse of my reflection in a shop window. Were you intentionally drawing me down this serpentine route into the underbelly of San Patricio, daring me? How far would she go?

How far would I go?

I didn't know yet.

Your hands were jammed into your back pockets, elbows fanned out. Your shirt billowed then flattened with each breath of wind.

I thought again of shouting your name and imagined you stopping, slowly turning, and watching as I trotted toward you.

No.

We wound around another corner, banked on one side by an abandoned gas station.

You seemed to know exactly where you were going. There was no hesitation at intersections, no consulting of the hand-drawn map you always carried in your back pocket. You'd been this way before.

Then, quite suddenly, you swerved diagonally across the road, pulled your hands out of your pockets, and leaned them against a set of swinging doors. I glanced at the painted sign: El Burro Filosófico — and laughed aloud. How like you, Otto, to go blocks out of your way for the pleasure of entering such a place. You disappeared inside, and for an instant the heels of your boots showed beneath the swinging doors. I looked to either side, half expecting shadowy forms to begin heading toward me. But all I could see was an old man crouched on the far side of the street, selling peanuts in newspaper cones. Were you at this instant cupping your drink, casting one eye toward the door?

Would she?

"Duck your head!" Father shouted from where he was standing knee-deep in the water.

I'd floated away, torso encased in a bulky inner tube.

"Put your face in the goddamn water!"

The profanity was a clue to his escalating tension. I felt oddly calm as I tossed over each wave in my safety ring. The water was one place where his will and mine met on equal terms.

"Kick your feet! Let's see some locomotion!"

I smiled, gave a tentative slap and jetted forward.

His face brightened. "The left leg. The left leg!"

He was striding toward me now, excited, scooping water back with cupped hands.

I closed my eyes and rolled belly-up. When I kicked I kicked only sky. The sun grilled my eyelids and a million diamonds sprinted across the horizon.

His hands beat the water. "No, Simone! No!"

"You do this on purpose, don't you, just to drive me crazy."

I pushed the ring over my head and looped it on the dock mooring. "Now why would I do that?"

I didn't follow you that day, Otto.

But I could have. It was precisely the sort of thing I would do. When I saw you hover in the doorway of the hardware store I did step back into the shadows, and in the next half-minute, as you fooled with your cigarette and hat, and folded peso bills into your wallet, I imagined the whole scene, feeling the cobblestone under my feet give way to rutted dirt, and the shiver of fear as you paused to knock something out of your shoe ... What if you glanced back? I saw you inside the dark cantina holding your hand out for a drink, and I even tasted the first bite of *mezcal* on your tongue.

Would she?

13

"EXCUSE ME. HELLO. How are you doing?"

I looked up, shading my eyes, expecting to see another young man wanting to practice his English.

But it was Geraldo standing there, dressed in a white shirt, jeans, and mirror sunglasses.

"Fine," I managed to say.

He motioned toward the space next to me on the bench and I quickly made room, pushing the webbed bags of groceries between my legs.

I'd never seen him in town and he looked entirely different, the sullen gaze vanished.

I waited for him to ask about Bob, but instead he peered into the tops of my bags.

"You like avocado?"

I did.

"You make *guacamole*?"

"Sure."

He seemed impressed, and I didn't have the heart to say I'd been eating it since I was two years old. Even the IGA in Rupert sold avocados and limes.

There was an awkward silence. Geraldo kept looking around the square and moving his legs, shifting position. When he caught my glance he'd smile nervously. A couple of teenage girls perched on the lip of the fountain were watching our conversation with great interest. Every time Geraldo spoke they dissolved into giggles.

"So," he said at last, "do you like San Patricio?"

I assured him I did, that it was very beautiful, very interesting. He nodded, but not as if he were really listening. The sun poured over us, and I wished I'd worn sunglasses too, feeling myself squint until my eyes were slits.

He beat his hands against his thighs a few times, then said abruptly, "Tomorrow is my sister Luisa's birthday. She is sixteen. We are having a fiesta at my family's house. I hope you can come."

I straightened. He was inviting me to his sister's birthday party, to his home.

Then I watched as he tore the flap off a packet of cigarettes and scribbled down an address. This he handed to me with a dazzling smile.

"You want *me* to come?" I said, making sure I'd got it right. Maybe he'd meant Bob.

"Please." Already he was getting to his feet.

"What time?"

He shrugged. "Eight o'clock."

The girls watched his easy saunter across the plaza and tittered behind cupped hands.

I told Bob first, catching him on his way back from the woodpile. One hand pressed half a dozen logs to his chest while the other clutched his tequila glass. He dumped the wood outside his door and watched as a giant spider skittered away.

"Know what this is all about?"

"What?"

"He's trying to prove to his family he's not queer. Invite the pretty *gringa* from up on the hill. Show them what a sharp customer he is. Then he'll settle down with a nice

Catholic girl and make babies." Without another word Bob entered his house, slugging tequila at twice his normal pace.

I was half hoping you'd talk me out of it.

"Don't you think it's funny he didn't invite you?" I said.

You laughed good-naturedly. "What would they want with an old fart like me? Go along; have a ball."

This wasn't quite the response I wanted. "My Spanish is so crummy ..."

"Who cares?" You waved this protest aside. "Don't you see, Simone, it's a privilege to be invited into this boy's home. A great opportunity to see how he lives. Go for it!"

So then, of course, I had to.

You drove me to number 15, Calle Bravo — an inauspicious wooden door set into the long crumbling wall that fronted the street. There was a sticker pasted just beneath the knocker reading ESTE HOGAR ES CATÓLICO.

I slipped out of the cab of the truck wearing a red miniskirt and black vest. Suddenly you became solicitous: leaning out the window, you ran over the arrangements again. We were to meet outside the house at twelve midnight — "On the dot, please."

"Will I turn into a pumpkin?"

"Very funny. Have a good time."

"I will." I kissed you quickly on the mouth.

When you drove away, the big wheels bumping over cobblestone, I felt a surge of excitement. Finally I was doing something on my own.

I rapped on the door and it was opened, after what seemed like forever, by a stout, middle-aged woman dressed in black.

She looked at me blankly, obviously wondering who I was. I explained, in my halting Spanish ... *Geraldo* ... *cumpleaños de Luisa* ... then let my arms hang at my sides. I must have got the address wrong, or the time. Possibly everything.

Finally the woman's mouth cracked into a smile. She started nodding furiously — but not opening the door further, and not beckoning me in. She was pointing at her watch.

"*A las diez.*"

Ten o'clock. It was only nine. I thought I'd arrived fashionably late.

The next half-hour was spent cruising the plaza, feeling self-conscious in my short skirt. Cars slowed down, and men muttered as they passed. Finally, for refuge, I ducked into Las Flores for one of their Nescafé cappuccinos, which came with two lozenge-shaped cookies. I downed these greedily. I sensed disapproval from the waiter, Beto's son, even as he flirted shamelessly, standing by my table after he'd delivered the coffee, darting looks down the front of my vest. I wasn't, after all, with my *novio*. Did I want to go dancing? he asked finally. I peered at my watch primly, as if I had an urgent appointment. No thanks, not today. Then I laughed. It *was* funny, these little cultural sidesteps, dark holes of misunderstanding. And I realized I was already composing the tale to tell you, Otto.

Stepping through the doorway I entered an open-roofed hall, its ceiling the darkening sky, the floor made of orange tile. I peeked through an opening to the left and saw a room with shuttered windows facing directly onto the street. Lying on a dark sofa was a thin, middle-aged man, perhaps asleep. TV light flickered across his face and I could hear women's voices and trickles of canned laughter.

"*Por aqui.*"

I was ushered toward the central courtyard by the woman I now understood to be Geraldo's mother. This terrace wasn't lush with bougainvillea, or decorated with squawking parrots in ornate cages as in the better hotels, or houses of the rich. The orange floor tiles continued and the courtyard was surrounded by unembellished concrete walls — perhaps seven feet high on the side flanking the neighbor's. Somebody had strung up lights but otherwise there was no obvious sign of festivity. Geraldo's mother, a short but broad woman whose shoulders strained against the material of her glittering blue dress, guided me to a straight-backed chair. It sat, one of many in a row that bisected the courtyard. Half a dozen guests were already there, sitting quietly, balancing plastic cups on their laps. Moments later a child brought me my own cup full of orange fizzy liquid; Fanta, I guessed, taking a delicate sip. Laced with Bacardi. The other women were all much older than me. Grannies or aunts. They smiled, watching me drink, then went back to their conversation. Where was Geraldo? And where — I looked around for signs of a sixteen-year-old-girl — was Luisa? All I could see were the old people, and half a dozen quiet children.

For an hour I continued to sit on the hard-backed chair, getting slowly drunk on the sugary punch and growing more hungry by the minute. There was no food, not even a bowl of chips. None of the guests roved around; once they were seated they stayed put. It felt like a doctor's waiting room. The women chatted while the men, dressed in clean shirts and cotton pants, didn't say a word. They perched on their chairs, cradling their plastic cups, and stared straight ahead.

When could I politely leave, I wondered.

"No food at all?" I could hear you say, nodding your head with sympathy.

"Not a scrap."

I smiled. Imagining how I would tell the story was much more fun than the event itself.

Then, finally, I sniffed happily. A delicious smell was issuing from a room at the opposite end of the courtyard. I would wait a little longer. The sky had darkened and with it the air had cooled. I shivered inside my meager clothing and wished I'd thought to bring a shawl. The only light now came from the string of lights and the glow of cigarettes. In the distance a siren wailed from the town's only ambulance.

Geraldo's mother emerged from the room at the back, wiping her hands on a checked apron, and motioned for me and six others to follow her into the kitchen.

A long wooden table had been set with spoons, napkins, and cans of Pepsi. We took our seats silently, four men and two women. Geraldo's mother, aided by a girl of perhaps eight, set down bowls of steaming *pozole* at each place. There was no conversation, beyond nods of thanks. Crusty rolls were passed around in a basket while we struggled with the tabs of our soft drink cans. Eating was performed efficiently and seemingly without joy. Within four or five minutes the guests began to finish and one by one they got up, muttered "*Gracias*," and passed their empty bowls to the little girl, who instantly began to wash them in a bucket.

I gulped fast. There was no time to linger; already the next shift was appearing at the door, waiting to be seated.

"Nobody spoke?" you prodded.

"Not a soul."

Even as I wiped my chin I was forming the conversation, adding those sharp observations you loved: the soup simmering in a huge clay *olla* on top of the two-burner stove while above, a hand-tinted photo of the Virgin scrutinized the diners. We ate from bowls made of some kind of translucent china, tinged with orange. The walls were stucco, fissured with long, complicated cracks, and there was absolute silence, except for the clank of cutlery.

"Where was the birthday girl?"

Good question.

And where was Geraldo?

I checked my watch. Already 11:15. You'd be at the door in forty-five minutes.

My tablemates were collecting jackets and purses, heading toward the front entrance. The party, it seemed, was over. I'd have to hang around outside for three-quarters of an hour, or find my way back to the plaza and pray for a cab.

Suddenly, bursting through the doorway with loud whoops and giggles came a crowd of young people. They filled the hall, edging politely past the departing guests, and in the lead was Geraldo, hailing me with both arms over his head.

"You are here already!"

The courtyard was instantly transformed. Chairs were whisked away and a pair of giant speakers were planted at opposite walls. Somebody poured bags of potato chips into an immense bowl. A tall man in a University of Colorado sweatshirt tucked a tape into the boom box then cranked it up so high that I felt the bass line tug the edges of my scalp. He turned to me and made the thumbs-up sign.

"Okay?"

"Okay!"

I was swept into the middle of the crowd, introduced in passing to Miguel, Ana, Patricio, Helena, Adolfo ... names shouted above the din of rock music. And then the dancing began. No one asked; I and the other girls and women were simply tossed from the arms of one young man to the next. Slim bodies and damp hands pressed against my hips and I felt weightless, some sort of airborne agent. As the evening wore on the young men peeled open their shirts and exposed slick, hairless chests. I slipped off my shoes and instantly wore holes in my tights. The music pounded, one song identical to the next. The girl in the iridescent blue blouse and skintight jeans was Luisa, and she danced fanning her hands out to either side as if she were drying her nail polish. She looked twenty, not sixteen.

The grannies and aunts and uncles and children had vanished into the darkness.

I didn't think of you Otto, not once.

You'd slid out of the house, disappeared with the stiff-backed chairs and grannies.

Then suddenly Geraldo switched off the music and the courtyard — for a breath's length — went silent. In that moment we all stood swaying, unable to let go of the music, feeling it trail through our fingertips. The world of San Patricio seeped back into the house; howling dogs, a band playing far off in the hills, a rooster crowing. The air felt deliciously cool against our overheated bodies.

Quick consultations, a visit to the punch bowl, and then we were pressing down the hallway and heading into the night. Twenty young people covered both sidewalks and the cobblestone street between. We marched with arms slung over each other's shoulders, laughing, chattering, and singing. Geraldo's hand gripped my shoulder and sometimes our hips clanged together. But it was the young man with the batik T-shirt that he watched — dancing just ahead in his high-top sneakers, hair tucked into a ponytail.

We angled left, took another left, until I had no idea where we were. There was sparse lighting in San Patricio outside of the main square. Shops that during the day were simply doors stamped into walls were now open, showing dimly lit bakeries or cantinas. We stopped at a door that was little more than a hatchway, with a handmade sign reading Café Alegría painted over its portal.

In single file we ducked our heads and made our way down the stairs into a tiny cellar room which we instantly filled. Everyone greeted a young bearded man whose eyes lit up when we entered.

His name was Gino, Geraldo explained, a Peruvian musician who'd fled Lima one night while the police banged on his door. Our group took over the tiny café, topping up the cappuccino machine, tearing cellophane off a tray of pastries, and lighting candles. Drums and guitars and mandolins were pulled off wall hooks and handed around. I got a small drum and a wooden mallet. Soon everyone had mugs of hot frothy coffee and something to bang on or pluck. We sang — Mexican tearjerkers and American pop songs, then took turns performing solos. When it was my turn, I sang, a cappella, the tune Father launched into when he hit the home stretch on the highway: "I'm just a rolling stone, all alone and lost ..."

The party was over. My new friends disappeared into the night, after handshakes — an odd formality — leaving just Geraldo, Luisa, and myself to return to the house.

I remembered I had a watch and looked at it: 1:45 in the morning. There was a twinge of remorse, but it didn't last long. I was too happy. As we walked silently down the street, all conversation over now, all singing exhausted, the only sign of human life was an old man crouched by a brazier, its coals glowing in the darkness. Shreds of unnamed meat were pushed to one side of the grill.

You were perched on the back fender of the truck in front of the house, puffing furiously at a cigarette.

"Otto!"

Stony silence.

As we drew closer Luisa whispered, "¿*Tu papa?*"

Your face in the glow of the cigarette was severe and unforgiving. I saw you through their eyes and realized that you looked *old*, Otto. For the first time I was embarrassed, even ashamed. You rose, very slowly, rounded the cab of the truck, and popped open the driver's door. After hastily making my goodbyes I dropped into the seat next to you. The key was already in the ignition, you'd already begun to steer into the street. I sank back, sighing, meaning to sound happy, meaning you to hear it.

We got as far as the foot of our hill before you spoke.

"Where were you, Simone?"

I pretended not to hear your annoyance and, without apology, told you where I'd been. My voice rose and fell with a fraction too much expression, too obvious a performance of happiness. You stared ahead into the darkness as I chattered on. A swampy smell from the *barranca* drifted through the windows as we climbed the twisting slope.

"The fellow with the mandolin had apparently sung with —"

"Never" — you interrupted my monologue — "do that to me again."

I stopped, chilled by your tone. "Do what?"

"Terrify me."

I felt all the joy of the evening capsize.

"I had no idea where you were. I knocked on the door,

the neighbor's door — and no one answered. There wasn't a goddamn sound, not a human to be seen. How the hell was I supposed to know you'd waltzed away with your pals to some hippie café?"

I didn't say anything.

"You could have been hauled off and raped for all I knew." Your voice was barely a whisper. "I was already composing the phone call to your parents. Telling them how I'd let you go to some party with people I knew nothing about —"

"Is that what you were scared of?" I interrupted. "Having to make a tough phone call? Well, I'm sorry to have put you through that."

You braked and turned toward me. "Shut up!"

My mouth opened, speechless at last.

"You know nothing. Nothing." Deep creases ran up your cheeks; your skin was dry and gray. The hands lacing the wheel were freckled, tufted with hair. I thought of the boys I'd danced with — their smooth skin and open smiles.

"Don't you see ...? I can't let this happen."

"Can't let what happen, Otto?" Something had shifted; I felt removed, distant, and bone tired from all the dancing and singing.

You didn't answer — but, perhaps because I wasn't trying, I understood. You were afraid of me, of how I'd made you feel.

What was the beloved wearing?

How did he seem — a trifle sad, perhaps?

Was there a boy with him?

Bob trailed after me as I took my morning mug of coffee to the end of the veranda. His cavernous cheeks sprouted gray bristles and he hadn't bothered to comb his hair. I got the idea he'd been hanging around since dawn, pacing up and down the veranda, waiting for me to wake up. My head burned from all the sweet punch.

"Was there a boy?" he repeated.

"I'm not sure."

He followed me to the clay wall that divided our row of houses from the ravine. In the dry season — now — it served as a garbage dump. Whiffy at the best of times, this morning it seemed unbearable. Yellow dogs rooted amongst the debris, discovering breakfast.

" 'I'm not sure'!" Bob repeated with a snort. "You can do better than that."

His neediness was creepy. His neediness, I realized in one of those rare moments of clear perception, was utterly familiar.

The binoculars hang from a nail hammered fifteen years ago by the window — part of a plan to keep tabs on bird migration patterns. I'd spent hours peering through them, adjusting focus, pretending to observe the feeding habits of a Baltimore oriole or snowy owl, when in fact I was watching the boys ride up the ridge on their bikes. They'd strip to their shorts, then leap in pairs off the cliff.

Like those divers we saw in Acapulco, only these boys don't know there's an audience.

If Nicky splits his head open on the rocks, who will be witness but me? Who will race to town and tell his parents? That nice man with the worried face who gave me a ride home once when it was raining. I've rehearsed this task in my mind, how I will be plainspoken and avoid phrases like "passed away" or "deceased."

"I'm sorry to tell you your son was killed while diving from the cliff. A deadly miscalculation, a matter of inches."

I will not giggle nervously.

"I can describe exactly how he looked the instant before his death." I'll allow myself to be invited into the little frame house, where tea will be poured with shaking hands, cookies passed around, the conventions of hospitality clung to. Everything will be shades of beige, except for one leather-covered chair in the corner, equipped with a footstool. On the coffee table will be one of those bound books with raised gold lettering: OUR GUESTS.

"He was extraordinarily beautiful, his back arched, arms pushed straight ahead, eyes wide open, as if he knew what was coming."

At that their eyes will shadow. I'd gone too far.

But they will ask me to stay on, to talk of their son whom they knew only in parts, not his angel half.

PART THREE

PART THREE

Very rarely is the beloved more than a shaping
spirit for the lover's dreams. And perhaps such
a thing is enough. To be a muse may be enough.
The pain is when the dreams change, as they do,
as they must. Suddenly the enchanted city fades
and you are left alone again in the windy desert.

Jeanette Winterson, *Sexing The Cherry*, 1989

14

IT WAS DURING the solar eclipse, and all three of us huddled on the cabin roof, safety film in hand. The universe darkened, and a chill rolled across the valley. How dark could it get? There were no shadows, only this pervasive gloom. Father balanced a stopwatch and clipboard on his knee.

"What if it stays like this?" Mother said. "If the sun never reappears?" Her voice sounded calm and interested.

"We'd all die," Father replied. "Photosynthesis would shut down."

Suddenly the wait became unbearably tense.

I remembered what he'd said about closed spaces, and how when the office elevator hovered too long before the doors opened, he'd start nervously jabbing the Open button. Who was to say that just because a thing works ten times or a hundred, it will again?

Your thumb dug gently into the notch at the top of my spine and massaged the little hollow. I felt myself float, as if by pressing down you were also lifting me into the air, and I hung taut as a kite on a string. Your legs sprawled straight out, your boots had been shucked off, and I watched your little toe poke from a hole in your sock. Such a toe! With its crusty nail, the hard yellowed skin built into sedimentary layers after years of scuffing leather.

"This," you sighed, "is perfect." The massage stopped, and I felt myself hover dangerously slack. "To sit here and feel your body. And the best part is" — you paused, reflecting, — "that I feel no sense of possession, no need, no desire to own you."

I nodded wisely and ignored the twinge of disappointment.

"Do you know what a breakthrough that is?" You pushed me away just enough to get a good look at my face. "I couldn't just 'sit' with Carmen, not without my scrabbling, picking at the moment, worrying how long it would last. Wondering — What does that distracted look *mean*? Do I believe that story about the busted muffler? I'll make some lame excuse and slip away, glance under the rear fender ...

"It's a disease, Simone, the parasite of jealousy, which digs your insides, files you down from the inside out."

You wanted to stroke every inch of my body, first with your hands, then your tongue, yet whenever I reached with my own hand you pushed it away. "No," you murmured, "I want to do this." So I fell back onto the bed as you meticulously unbuttoned my blouse and slipped it off, first one sleeve, then the other. I was naked; you were fully clothed, like characters in some Renaissance painting.

Next morning I awoke, feeling the bed lurch as you rolled off it. The fire was a cluster of wood fragments, but you didn't kneel, as usual, to toss in fresh kindling. Instead you strode toward the mock Colonial bureau, wrestled the drawer open, shook out your red shirt — the one with Western style pockets — and laid it on the bed. You folded the sleeves toward the middle, then expertly flipped the tails under. Your hands, I noticed, were shaking, and you didn't glance up once to see if I was awake. You snatched two pairs of undershorts and dropped them on top. Then, rooting through the pile of clothes on the chair, you found a pair of black jeans and slipped into them, leaving the buckle and top button undone. You set out for the bathroom and returned ten minutes later, smelling of soap and holding a tuft of toilet paper to your chin. Still you hadn't uttered a word. You yanked the knapsack off the shelf and dropped it onto the bed, then stood staring at it, hands flexing, the dot of blood on your chin seeping through the tissue.

"Going somewhere?" I hauled myself to a sitting position.

For a long time there was no reply, and I almost repeated the question.

"Yes," you said finally. "I guess I am."

It was the dead way you spoke that soaked me with dread.

"I guess I am," you repeated, still flexing your hands. "To Mexico City." You snapped out of the dreamy tone, reached for the clothing, and stuffed each piece into the sack. "I need to get away."

My feet touched the floor. I'd pulled the coarse blanket over my shoulders. The room was icy.

You didn't look at me. "A relationship needs air. There's something wrong if I can't feel free to do this."

"Air?" My feet searched for sandals.

"Space." You grabbed a pair of socks and dropped them into the bag. "Elbow room."

My head was spinning. "I can give you any space you need, Otto."

"'*Give me*'?" You took a breath and let it out slowly. "That's just the problem. It's not a matter of me asking and you giving. It should be already there, built into the system, not software but hardware."

You zipped up the sack and fastened the straps.

"I know that," I said.

"Listen ..."

"Do I have a choice?"

A pained look. "I feel you've been —"

"Been *what*, Otto?" The blender in my stomach whipped its blades. "Are you punishing me for the other night?"

You pretended not to understand.

"With Geraldo," I prompted, hugging myself with the thick goaty blanket. Bob was fooling with his shortwave radio next door, picking up some cracker preacher from Texas: "*Ah tell you that when it's time to enter the Kingdom ...*"

Bob had a religious streak; he would invite the Jehovah's Witnesses into his house while he searched for money.

"Of course not," you said at last. You sounded put out, as if such a notion was too silly to consider. "Did you honestly think we could continue week after week like this?"

"Like what?"

"You claim you want to enter the world fully, but you're scared of the first shred of reality —" You stopped, checked your pockets for visa and wallet, and resumed. "And you want me to say something now, to make it better — don't you?"

I let the blanket fall open so you could see me shivering.

"All I need is two or three days solo. You're not afraid of being alone, are you? Bob's next door. I'll speak to him."

"Don't. That's not it."

For a minute your words got mixed up with the radio voice: "*When the sky darkens, the birds are silent, and you are seized with an unholy terror ...*"

"I could ride with you." I pounced on the idea. "When we get there we wouldn't have to stay in the same room; I could even go to a different hotel. I could ..."

You held up your hand and began to back away.

"It could be fun!" My voice rose a notch.

"If this relationship is so fragile —"

I stood up then, knowing only that I must not allow you to finish the sentence. You took another step back and eyed me warily, as if I were an animal you weren't sure about. I reached out and hooked an arm around your middle and drew you toward me, then began to knead each vertebra in turn, inching toward the top of your jeans. You stiffened but I pressed on, digging under your pants for the knot of tailbone.

"Not now, Simone."

Your mouth was a chamber I knew well; my tongue dove deep while I reached below and fit my hand between your legs. Even as you protested, your lower body sank into mine.

I mopped up with my blouse. You watched this for a moment, then tugged the garment from my hands and began to scrub your own belly with quick, energetic strokes.

"I'm going." You tossed the soiled blouse onto the bed and reached for your jeans.

I stared, disbelieving.

"What am I supposed to do here?" Semen was drying on my face, puckering the skin.

"Anything you want." You sounded bored and fed up.

How would I taste, or touch, without you to show me how? I'd become so used to your instructions that I couldn't imagine the bleakness of myself alone in a landscape. How could I *see*? The emptiness gaped, terrifying in its intensity.

"Get something on; you'll catch a cold."

"What will I do here?" I persisted.

"For God's sake." You pulled on a threadbare sweatshirt. "Don't do this to me; don't do it to yourself." You started for the front door.

I watched, frantic.

"Wait! Where will you stay?"

Your shoulders slumped. "I haven't decided."

"I'll get the guidebook!" I skated across the tile toward my studio. You would thank me for this. Sometimes, when I was pretending to work in there, I was really planning trips, checking off points of interest, restaurants and hotels I thought you might like. I scooped the volume off my table and raced back to the hall.

You weren't there.

"Otto?" my voice shrilled. "*Otto!*"

"Right here." You were standing by the front door, sack slung over your shoulder, hand fooling with the latch.

I pressed the book into your free hand. "You'll find an excellent selection on —"

"Please, Simone ..." You started backing out. "Let me go." The chunky guidebook dropped to the floor.

I HAVE REACHED FOR LOW SPIKED SHRUBS THAT WERE DISGUISED AS HANDHOLDS

This was printed in bold letters on the wall above your worktable. When I reached out to touch the words they streaked. Now you'd guess I'd been here. Of course you knew me better than I knew myself, and whatever patch of highway you were barreling down, you were nodding smugly, picturing me in here, hovering over your things, grasping for clues.

This was where you worked: the Kingdom of Art. A pile of blank paper, an unglazed mug full of sharpened HB pencils, and taped to the wall a series of seemingly careless drawings, squiggles that I often seeked to imitate.

HANDHOLDS — to what? To heave you from despair and loneliness? Was this something you'd copied from a book, or had you invented it, scratching the words on paper, then, with a little giggle of delight, taping it to the wall?

I'd been in this room many times, of course, but never alone. Now I could crack open any notebook, lift the piles of paper, skim through the scraps of notes with quotations, scrawled ideas, half-formed sketches — this was my chance. What is it you did in here hour after hour, day after day?

LOW SPIKED SHRUBS — was this me, the "spiky shrub" when you'd longed for a helping hand?

I backed out without opening a box or lifting a single piece of paper. Not out of honor, Otto, or any respect for privacy — but because I was scared out of my wits. I was convinced you'd set a trap; hairs between sheets of paper, carefully situated crumbs that would float unnoticed to the ground — so that the instant you returned you would know. And then, would you not have a perfect right to despise me?

☀ 15 ☀

"YOUR BOYFRIEND took off in a hurry."

I started. It was Bob, coming up the veranda stairs, balancing a load of firewood and a coffee cup.

I quickly recomposed my face. "He's driven into Mexico City for a few days."

Bob dumped the wood and took a slug of coffee. "Sucker could've let me know. There's a package sitting at the U.S. Consulate with my name on it, and I got no money to travel."

"It was a sudden decision. You know how it is; a relationship needs air."

"Air." Bob looked at me sharply.

"A relationship has its own rhythm and punctuation," I continued, improvising, but confident that some part of you was gazing on with approval. "Its need for commas and colons — otherwise it just runs on till it's out of breath."

"Only thing is," Bob said, "I want to be the guy writing the script, putting in those periods and commas and what-have-yous."

On Sunday we always read *The News*, the English-language newspaper, with its endless reports of parties in the ex-pat communities. The kiosk on the main plaza brought in exactly six copies, one for Bob, one for us, and the rest for tourists passing through.

"Look at this character's hand," I heard your voice as clearly as if you were sitting beside me on the bench. I peered at the blurry photo: various men in suits at a reception for the Ballet Folklórico.

"He's protecting his nuts."

"From what?" I squinted.

"Look harder, dear."

I did, then saw what you'd spied immediately: a fragment of another photo had been superimposed on this one. The faint tracing of a machine gun was pointed directly at the man's groin, and, coincidentally, his hand was down there, splayed protectively.

"I see it," I grinned. Yet you weren't there, or anywhere near me. By now you'd be halfway to the capital.

Then who was it that was seeing?

And whose voice had I heard?

Your right hand moved hastily while the other steadied the paper. You thought I was reading the menu: *Sopa de Fideos*.

What were *fideos*? Some kind of bean?

I'd never seen you do this before, make a spontaneous, realistic sketch — for hadn't photography superseded realism? And drawings of "local color" were too corny for words.

I lowered the menu, and at the same instant you recognized what you'd done. Your hand curled around the paper, crushing it thoroughly, and you gave it a toss toward the green can marked BASURA.

Nothing was said. But for the first time, Otto, I seriously doubted. The gesture seemed ridiculous, not "tough" or intelligent, but fearful, as if one inconsistent act threatened your whole enterprise.

I began to draw from my favorite bench on the San Fernando square just off the marketplace. You were miles away, and almost immediately I felt the return to some essential activity, natural as breathing.

First I drew the awning over the fruit-seller's booth, then the pyramids of oranges and avocados, and the girl sitting by a table spread with tiny piles of seeds. You were right, I told myself. We did need a break from each other.

"What are the chances of getting beaned by a chestnut if I sit here?" I positioned myself on an outstretched towel under the tree.

Father gazed speculatively up at the laden branches, then at me, or, to be more specific, at my skull. Judging circumference and total area of exposure.

Already I regretted my words.

"First we'd have to calculate the number of chestnuts, and wind velocity, then divide by —" To my surprise he stopped mid-sentence, pursing his lips.

"Damned if I know," he grunted, still squinting into the sun.

My father, after barely a second's pondering, had given up. And to boot, he seemed not the least irritated. Instead he yawned widely and said, "Sometimes it's best not to think about these things."

There was an insistent tapping on the door, and I jumped: we rarely had visitors and Bob never bothered to knock. He'd stroll in without any greeting and embark on the endless free-flowing monologue of his life. Sometimes you looked up from what you were doing and said, "Not now, Bob," and he'd back out, still chattering, waving his drink for emphasis.

"¿Hola? ¿Simona?" a woman's voice called.

I recognized it right away and swung open the door. Adela, resplendent in a topaz-colored blouse and skintight jeans, granted me a *beso* on each cheek before entering the house. She didn't conceal her curiosity, peering into the kitchen, then at the sketch pad left open on the table.

"You did this?"

I nodded yes.

"It's very good." She paused a long time to look at the drawing. "You draw real things, not like your friend. This" — she pointed to the picture — "I understand. And I like, very much." She leaned in close, scanning the page for details. "I know her; she is the grandmother of my friend." She tapped the face of the old herb-seller.

I felt faintly embarrassed. This was not the recognition I craved.

"It's just a rough sketch. I made it for fun."

"But you must frame it, take it to the little museum next to the convent —"

"No, no."

She looked at me sharply. "Who cares what he thinks."

I had to smile. "Can I get you something? A cold drink?"

"Please."

I began bustling around the kitchen, squeezing oranges into glasses. Soon we were both installed on canvas chairs in the courtyard, cradling juice spiked liberally with rum. It was just before five in the afternoon and the shadows had begun to deepen. A bucket of foaming washwater sat in the corner. I'd been cleaning like mad and the air smelled of ammonia and damp clay. I waited for her to ask where you were, so I could examine her face for any twinge of disappointment.

"Very nice." She closed her eyes briefly as the sun snuck out from behind a billowing cloud. Her blouse pulled across her chest as she adjusted position. The courtyard was entirely open to the sky and I was decked out in full protective gear: floppy hat and long sleeves, face thickly coated with sunscreen. Her head was bare, her skin dark and smooth.

Suddenly, for no reason I could fathom, she began to speak of a cousin called Mauro.

"He is young," she said, and looked at me pointedly. "Like you. Tomorrow afternoon he is teaching folk dancing at my school. You must come." Her tone allowed no space for argument.

"Sure," I said, knowing I wouldn't.

"Mauro is the best dancer in all the state; he has won every prize, every competition. And" — she leaned over and touched my knee softly — "he is *muy guapo*."

I lifted my eyebrows.

She looked pleased with herself, as if it were all settled.

"You should meet more Mexicans while you are here, Simona, not always stay up on the hill with your old gringo and" — she waved dismissively — "that *borracho* next door."

"I just went to a fiesta —"

"Yes, yes," her mouth pursed. "Geraldo. But Mauro is different; he likes girls."

I felt myself tighten. "Besides, my 'old gringo' isn't even here now, he's gone off to —"

"Mexico," she interrupted.

"How did you know?"

"He told me."

I watched a tiny insect with translucent wings dive-bomb the washwater. "When?"

She waved airily. "Days ago."

Days ago. So I'd mapped it out all wrong. After being convinced that you'd woken up with a sudden attack of restlessness, here was proof that you'd been cooking up an escape for days. Face burning under the sunscreen, I took a gulp of juice, feeling the rum shoot to my head.

Adela chattered on. "'Look in on Simona,' he asked me, and so today I come to see how you are and if you are lonely."

She reached to give me a maternal pat, and I saw, to my mortification, that my hand was clenched into a claw on my lap.

Look in on me? As if I were some elderly shut-in, some poor friendless half-wit reheating soup on the stove. The world tilted and my feet splayed to either side for balance. This was, as you'd often warned, earthquake country.

"Know who you remind me of?" You leaned in, face huge and smiling.

"Who?"

"Goldilocks."

"Come on, Otto."

"She lies on the first bed but it's too big and lumpy, so she slides onto the next. Too soft. Ever optimistic, she drops onto the third bed, bounces a few times, hauls her legs up and — Eureka — a perfect fit. What happens next?"

"She falls asleep."

"Precisely." You looked smug. "That's what happens when you get too comfortable. Then" — you leaned in — "the bears come home."

☀ 16 ☀

I'D BEEN EXPECTING the sound all day, yet when the crunch of tires signaled your arrival I did not leap to my feet like an eager puppy. Instead, I listened to the cough of motor as it sputtered to a stop. It was hard to get unleaded gas down here. I'd been yawning a lot, catching up on oxygen after so many weeks of anxious, shallow breathing. (You were right; the relationship needed air.) I coasted across the veranda and waited on the steps while you popped open the door of the truck and began to lope toward me. Your eyes had a fixed, slightly wary look.

"You're back," I said. I wasn't going to make it easy.

You stopped, then, with an elaborate gesture, like a circus emcee, swept one arm back toward the truck. The door on the passenger side pushed open and a woman stepped out, cautiously finding her footing on the uneven ground. She was North American, dressed entirely in black, a style that looked shockingly urban. Her dark hair was streaked with silver and her complexion was pale, almost white, except for red-glossed lips. Long slender fingers clutched a canvas bag by its strap. She stood a moment, leaning first one way, then the other, grimacing, while behind her a boy heaved himself out. He

looked about sixteen, dressed in jeans, high-tops, and a flannel
shirt. A wad of tangled hair stuck out from under a baseball hat.

"There they are!" you said, arm still aloft.

I smiled thinly and waited for an explanation.

"This is Carmen," you rocked back and forth on both
heels. "And our son, Kip."

Carmen. Your wife. Ex-wife. Or "ex-life," as you once
termed her.

"Welcome to San Patricio," I heard myself say, then
reached to shake their hands, first her small cool one, then the
boy's reluctantly offered tug.

"So that's the real reason you went into Mexico City," I said in
a tight voice. We were fixing snacks, which meant I was
holding the tray while you loaded it with glasses and plates.
Your family waited outside. Bubbling on the stove was the
meal I'd prepared in anticipation of your arrival.

You avoided my glance. "I'm afraid so." But you
couldn't contain your joy. Sniffing happily at the simmering
pot you said, "Think we can stretch it?"

"I wasn't expecting extra Guests." The pun was intentional.
"Why didn't you tell me?" I followed you to the cupboard.

Hefting a thick clay bowl you said, "She wrote me she
was bringing the boy. I haven't seen him for months." Your
eyes held mine. "Do you have any idea how tough it is to tell
you something you don't want to hear?"

I froze.

You seized a bottle opener and dropped it onto the tray.
"This is my *family*, Simone."

"And are you liking it here?" Carmen was peering down her
nose at me.

I heard myself answer in a bizarre Southern drawl
that, yes, I certainly was.

She squinted. "Where did you say you were from?"

"Good question," you muttered.

I snapped the beer caps open and started pouring so energetically that foam rose and immediately drenched the tabletop.

"Jesus, Simone!" You grabbed the glasses and wiped them clean.

You hadn't touched me yet, I realized, not even a comradely peck of greeting. What was I supposed to be then — a student? Girlfriend? Travel buddy? You could have warned me, Otto. I fastened onto this indignity, convincing myself it was the real reason I felt so rotten. It was your lack of faith, not the deed itself that stung.

Carmen pulled up her legs until she was crouching, yoga position, on the chair. Her minute waist was cinched by a studded belt that must have been six inches wide. How could she breathe, I wondered.

"Has it changed?" Your arm took in the house, the veranda, the whole valley.

"It's scruffier," she said. "When we were here there was a guy tending to the grounds."

"Don —"

"Ernesto," she filled in.

My face kept a rigid smile. Don't let them know; that was what mattered most of all. To take it in stride. I clung to this decision, my whole body coiled in effort.

"This is where our son was conceived." She was looking at me again with that slightly bemused expression.

"I know," I said, not losing a beat. "Otto told me."

"I'm glad he told you something."

You laughed nervously, then abruptly rose to perch beside Kip on the railing. Your laugh went on and on, and the boy stiffened, yet you continued, determined not to let our silence intimidate you. I could see over your shoulder to the lake below, pulsing with heat. A lone ferry crept across its shimmering skin: a trip we'd been meaning to make since our first week in San Pat.

Carmen reached into her bag, drew a slender cigar from a case, and waited. Suddenly you were fishing around in your pockets, hunting for matches. You located a scruffy packet, leaned forward, and snapped one match against your fingernail.

It didn't light.

You tried the next.

Same thing.

Carmen just waited with fixed patience, gazing over your head at the stucco wall. With each match your hand began to tremble more, and it was only after half a dozen that you were successful, cupping the fragile flame and touching it to the tip of the cigar while she inhaled.

She stretched her legs, pressed her toes against the heel of one boot, and tugged. Effortlessly, the boot slipped off, revealing a perfectly arched foot sheathed in black nylon. You stared, chewing your lower lip. You must have, hundreds of times, reached for that ankle and held it in your hands, then bent to smooth your cheek against the delicate instep.

Then you were looking at me, not with irritation — but recognition. You'd seen your own stare mirrored in my eyes. I felt my heart quicken, for once again our minds were in perfect accord. And moments later, when we found ourselves in the kitchen, I grabbed both your hands.

"She's gorgeous, Otto."

"Isn't she?" You looked concerned. "Of course, she's just here to drop off the kid, there's no question of —"

"Of course."

I handed your son a bottle of Corona. He was still perched on the railing, his cumbersome body and outsize clothes blocking my view of the lake.

"Thanks," he grunted. The curtain of hair parted and I got a glimpse of his face.

"Otto —" I turned. "He has your mouth, exactly."

The hair fell back into place.

Beaming, you slung an arm over his shoulder. "Good-looking boy, isn't he?" You tried to brush the hair away again but he bent over, shrinking from the gesture.

"Don't, man," he said in a low voice.

Don't, man. I was appalled, yet thrilled. He wanted less — not more.

You refused to catch on. Instead you hiked your arm back into place and added a generous squeeze.

Kip froze. He jammed his thumb into the neck of the beer bottle.

"Fifteen years old," you went on. "Conceived in high altitude, already halfway to the moon." You seized the peak of his cap and spun it around.

"Leave the boy alone." Carmen knocked an ash over the railing. Her voice sounded tired.

You became louder, more insistent. "I love this kid. Even when he's a shit. Even when he grinds up the music so the goddamn walls shake. And surly? I love surly."

Kip's knee started to jigger.

"I'm so bloody glad to have you here." Your voice was thick.

A line in Kip's jaw tightened. The silence was excruciating.

At last Carmen spoke. "You can drive me to the hotel now," and she began to slip back into her boots. The sun was easing down over the lake, bringing a customary chill to the air.

A look of panic crossed your face. "I won't hear of it. You just got here. And there's plenty of room ..."

She stood and adjusted her belt, ignoring your plea. "Kip, stay with your father or come with me — suit yourself."

"No!" You dropped to the floor and stood a few inches from her, chest heaving.

"Otto," she sighed. "Don't change the rules. I've brought the boy, and —" she nodded toward me.

I held my breath. You fought for control, then turned to your son, assuming a falsely hearty voice. "Well, Kipper, will you stay?"

The boy sank back. "I don't care," his voice barely audible.

I recognized the Polaroid snap of the sullen teenager, that glowering closed-in face. A faint beard shaded his chin and upper lip.

You smiled with relief and touched his shoulder. "I won't be long."

As you and Carmen headed for the truck the boy wiped his mouth and mumbled, "You his girlfriend, or what?"

"Or what," I repeated, and left him there alone on the veranda.

"Son? Where are you? I'd like you to bunk down in my studio."

You'd returned from town, a set look on your face. Your skin was pale and drawn, your eyes puffy. "Simone sleeps on the pull-out in her studio."

I did?

As Kip padded across the courtyard with a clean towel you whispered, "I don't want to hit him with our relationship just yet; the kid's been through enough." Then you shouted directions through the closed bathroom door.

"C means *caliente*, hot, not cold."

When he'd finished showering and was stretched out asleep in your studio, you let yourself drop into your favorite chair. The vein on your temple was pulsing. I opened my mouth, not yet knowing which of a dozen questions to begin with. Suddenly your eyes snapped open and you reached for your notebook.

"If this is the trajectory of a star's life cycle ..." You pressed a felt-tip marker to the paper and drew a long arc.

I crouched beside you adding, "And if you stretch it till it flattens ..."

Our voices imitated normalcy. We knew what to do in this mode — but something was missing; the familiar flare of two minds in sync, that hum of elation I could count on as we lofted above the ordinary world. Even as I talked and pointed, I knew I was straining, mimicking the past. The boy in the next room snored gently. After a few minutes you looked up at the wall and dropped the marker.

"Will you sleep with me tonight, Simone? Please?"

It smelled like goat under there, damp goat hair and semen. I crouched as still as possible, holding my hand to my mouth so that my breathing couldn't be heard.

"Anything wrong, Kip?" you said calmly, as if you hadn't just rolled off me with a groan, seconds earlier.

"My stomach feels weird."

"Did you puke?"

"I feel like I'm going to."

"I'll be right there."

The bed creaked as you swung your legs down. Was your cock still stiff, I wondered? Did you shield it discreetly with your hand? And was it possible he hadn't seen me under the hump of blanket? I still felt the pressure on my head where you'd hastily pushed me under, whispering, "Quick — duck!"

In my dream, not exactly dream, but the slow inching toward sleep accompanied by yelping faraway dogs, I watch your former wife from inside the cab of the truck as she leans over the windshield with a rag to remove the dried corpses of insects. As she lifts her arm her blouse cracks open and there is a flash of red bra — La Vie En Rose — with tiny stem straps and whisper-thin cups, and under each the milky skin strains. She shrugs her arm across and up and down and across again, her face inches from mine, yet looking not at me but at the task at hand. In the not-quite-dream I press my fingers effortlessly through the window, as if it were a soapy membrane, and whisk my hand into that gaping neckline to that heart-stopping, silky skin. I know exactly where to linger. Her look is at first startled and she stops her work, and in the not-quite-dream I feel my groin swell and tug against the jeans zipper. Your jeans.

At the entrance to the Cinema Paradiso, Kip and I stood back as you asked, in bad Spanish, for "*Kwa-tro bo-letos, por favor.*"
Four tickets.
"*¿Dos adultos y dos niños?*" The bored attendant peered over your shoulder at the rest of us.
Carmen tilted her head back and laughed.
We entered the theater, single file, and to my surprise I felt your hand reach for me in the dark, press against the small of my back and slowly trail downward, ending with a feather touch between my legs. Inches ahead, your ex-wife and son moved cautiously down the aisle, feeling their way for unexpected stairs.

"See this?" Father pointed to the photo of a snake in the pamphlet sent by Fish and Wildlife. "The massasauga rattler. People down the road say they found one near their privy."

"Why are you holding your legs up like that, dear?" The old lady frowned through tortoiseshell glasses.
My bare legs stretched straight out, hovering in the air like a couple of skis. I was perching on a wooden chair in the cottage of Miss Gooderham, an ancient cousin who came up to Lake Huron every summer.
"Like what?"
"Aren't you a funny girl."
She passed me another stale gumdrop while I listened hard for hissings and low-pitched rattles.

☀ 17 ☀

"I NEED COFFEE," Carmen announced, pushing through the front door. She was wearing a man's gray blazer, the usual leggings, and a metallic gray T-shirt. Her skin was stark white, unaffected by San Patricio sun.

"Hey, kiddo." She reached for Kip and tousled his hair, dislodging the earphones. But he didn't wince or push her away; he even smiled slightly.

"Coffee? I'll make it." I hurried to the kitchen and felt her watching, amused.

Your footsteps crossed the courtyard.

"That you, Carmen?"

I knocked four heaping spoonfuls of Uruapan coffee into the filter.

"Where can I fax Rita in Buenos Aires?" I heard the scrape of chairs across the patio floor. "Customs is holding up the Martinez prints."

You seemed to know what she was talking about. "The post office has a machine. What about Stan? Isn't he supposed to look after it?"

"You know what he says — 'Bribe the suckers!' "

"So, do it."

"'So, do it,'" she mimicked your tone perfectly. "Why should I pay off some petty bureaucrat and perpetuate the corruption?"

This, I thought, splashing boiling water onto the grounds, is a world I know nothing about.

"I don't have much time," she was saying. "I shouldn't even be here. I canceled that meeting with External and probably buggered up my chances of getting Embassy help."

You made apologetic noises.

The coffee dripped slow motion.

"Next week I fly to Stockholm for the curators' conference. I've spoken to Kip — he can stay here till the end of the month."

You said something in a low voice.

"No," she replied evenly. "No, Otto."

I brought in the tray and she scooped a mug with one hand and a teaspoon with the other.

"Kenny Argue's still coming around."

"That hack?" You drained Carnation into your cup.

"Leaving boxes of godawful slides."

"He's off the booze again?"

"Who knows?"

"Who cares?" you both chorused.

"I slotted the Choyce boys for early fall." Carmen helped herself to chips and guacamole. "They'll do some high-concept installation, perfect for the Europeans hanging around at festival time. Then I've booked Leslie."

"Leslie?" you said with evident surprise. "I thought she was in the nuthouse."

"She was. I dropped by her studio and the entire place is littered with religious symbols and one-eyed cats — and some terrific sculpture. Don't laugh, Otto, *Artforum* has a feature coming up, center spread."

"Jesus. Leslie." Then you turned to me. "She was a student of mine."

We were alone together for less than three minutes and I felt so self-conscious that when I swallowed, the sound seemed to echo. Carmen sat in the oversize chair with its leather back and hammered copper nails and smiled.

"I suppose you're an artist."

"Aspiring," I said quickly.

"Of course. That's the kind Otto likes best."

Silence again. I counted the seconds till you returned.

"Are you listening to me, son?"

You used a queer, beseeching voice that set my hair on end.

"I know it wasn't your idea to come here, but give me a chance."

Kip slouched in the chair with acorn-size headphones dug into his ears, his eyes half open. The relentless chug of bass leaked and filled the room.

"Do I have a choice?" he finally said.

Where your features and Carmen's were intricately formed and knowingly placed, Kip's face was such a paradigm of teenage ordinariness that it took my breath away. He may have had your mouth but he kept it relentlessly static, and his eyes were too close together.

("There's no such thing as ugly," you'd said once, referring to a concrete building on the outskirts of Monterey. "There is only the inattention of the viewer.")

Long spidery arms hung at his sides, and somewhere inside the massive jeans a pair of gangly legs held him up. But it was his feet that struck me. How could Carmen, with her delicate ankles and slender toes, have produced a being with such giant, graceless feet — not that I ever got to see them in their natural form. Kip never went anywhere, not even to the bathroom, without his size 13 Nike high-tops shuffling beneath.

I'd catch you eyeing him speculatively, even admiringly, and always with longing. In return he'd shrug and crank up the music.

I forced myself to include him in our conversations, despite his complete lack of response. Where I ached to shake him hard, I assumed a generous approach that gained your approval. Once, after I asked him what music he was listening to and he grudgingly replied, "Butthole Surfers," you leaned over to whisper, "He likes you, I can tell."

At lunch he prodded the taco with one finger, then slumped back into his chair.

"Don't you like it?" you said with tender concern.

I'd made the meal, your favorite: tortillas filled with shredded ham, stringy Oaxaca cheese, and plenty of *salsa picante*.

"It stinks."

"You've had tacos back home, Kip."

"Not like these."

"Why don't you at least try it?"

"Why doesn't she make normal food?"

There was a tense silence and I felt my cheek muscles snap up and down while I waited for you to make the brat apologize. Instead, you pushed your plate away and said in an even voice, "All right, son," and rose to make a peanut butter sandwich.

When I see you hover behind her, staring balefully at that shimmering halo of inky hair with its streaks of silver, I too am inhaling her scent, hypnotized by secret longing. I too want to dive into that hair with my face and cling to it, suck it deep into my throat.

When you struggle to light her cigar, hand knocking the air, the flame so wild you have to steady yourself and breathe slowly, I am that shaking hand, I am the hard knot in your throat that murders speech.

"You can't do this!" You shook your head hard, like you were clearing your ears.

"Yes I can, Otto." Carmen's tone was firm, yet weary. I hovered, about to enter the room.

"I won't let you go." You moved to block her exit and, doing so, blocked my way in.

"Let me?" She clasped your wrist, lifted it off the door frame, and slipped past easily.

"Bitch!"

You watched her walk away, then cried, "Need a ride?"

"No."

She moved easily, sure of your stare.

We watched her disappear down the hill, piece by piece.

"Know what that was about?" You sank against the wall and your chest looked thin and hollow under your T-shirt.

"What?"

"She wants ..."

I waited.

"A di-vorce." You pronounced the word as if it were foreign.

"Isn't that what you want?"

You winced. "Don't you understand, Simone — she's serious."

Usually when Carmen left, a great tension sprang from the air. We'd begin to plod through bits of household business, tidy up newspapers, wash dishes, figure out where the gas leak was coming from. That day I heard the brittle quality of our voices, as in a movie when the music suddenly stops and speech is too distinct.

☀ 18 ☀

"YOU LOOK TERRIBLE." I set my shopping bag down on the trail.
"Where have you been?" I realized I hadn't seen Bob in days.

He looked dourly pleased by my comment. His shirt
was torn and filthy and there was a gash along one shoulder
blade.

"In jail."

"Jail? What happened?"

Bob lowered himself onto a rock. A maguey cactus
rose behind him, whirring with tiny insects. "Geraldo is gone
— for good."

I waited. His stories always gave me goose bumps.
He'd have the latest town gossip: who'd put a slug in whose
brother, who'd been robbed, or got knocked up, or had his
skull kicked in by the police.

"The little sucker's gone and killed himself."

I heard, but didn't understand, not right away. "That's
impossible!" The image chimed once: Geraldo, shirt open, tucking
his fingers into the waistband of the boy with the ponytail.

Bob crossed one thin leg over the other. "Two nights
ago, he was driving with cousin Alfredo to Leon to visit the

whorehouse. The family decided he needed some girl action. Coming home, pecker-drained and drunk out of their minds —" Bob paused, anxious to get the sequence right. "They missed the goddamn curve, and Geraldo" — he took a breath and finished the sentence in precise tones — "shot through the windshield and got himself hung up on a cactus. He was always a religious boy."

I crouched on the rock beside him, feeling sick and hot.

"So I visited every cantina in town until they chucked me out, then hit on some off-duty cop packing a monster handgun left over from Pancho Villa's army ..." Bob's voice trailed off and he was silent a moment, lifting a cigarette to his mouth in elegant slow motion.

The kitchen table was littered with the shed skin of a mango. I smelled those cheap cigarettes that always made you cough. You were squeezing your temples with both hands, and the moment I walked in you straightened, showing a face drenched in disgust. "Do I *look* like such an idiot? Am I losing my mind?"

"I don't know," I said, dropping half a dozen miniature chocolate bars on the table. "What did you do?"

"If I told you" — one hand reached out to seize mine — "you'd be disgusted."

My skin burned with the heat of yours. "Try me." I would not tell you about Geraldo, I decided. I knew exactly what you'd say: "Poor kid," giving a brief, sympathetic wince.

"Don't you wonder why I took so long driving her back?"

"I hadn't noticed," I said, and for once, it was true.

"I waited till she went inside, then followed her into the lobby." You were watching me. "Then I kept going, up the stairs, after her."

"Did she know?"

"Of course not; but I just couldn't let go."

Up the chipped stone stairs with the ornate iron railing, past the landing with the stone urn, and the sepia portrait of Benito Juárez: we'd stayed in this hotel our first night in San Patricio.

"I was tiptoeing so she wouldn't hear, yet at the same time I think I wanted her to swing around. Have you ever done that? Tailed someone?" Your hand tightened over mine.

I pretended to think. "Maybe."

"Then you know. You're inches away from total degradation."

I saw you flattened against the tile wall, heart pounding as she enters the corridor to her room. She's dangling the key, copper colored, attached to a leather tag.

"When did she see you?" I said in a low, excited voice. "Did she glance around just before she slipped the key into the lock?"

"How did you know that?"

I shrugged modestly.

"So there I was, lurking in the shadows, breathing heavily like some lunatic, a woman's worst nightmare, dick popping out of my pants —"

"Did she scream?"

"Hardly. What she did was tilt her head back" — you demonstrated this — "and laugh." Then you laughed, a hard, forced sound.

I felt humiliation tear through my body. I felt it like a sudden cramp that doubles you up and leaves you gasping for air. And seconds later, when you tugged me onto your lap, I was the one who whispered "*Bitch*" and felt your whole body shiver.

☀ 19 ☀

THE PONIES TORE down the ridge, manes flapping, ears tugged back, and all we could do was cling as hard as we might and squint into the rush of hot midday air. If they stumbled we'd go flying over their heads, and that was the fun of it, not to know from second to second. We were in one of those gaucho stories by Borges, galloping through the dusty pampas — except you weren't with us, Otto. This was the day Carmen demanded you drive her to the airport, so I rode with your son, a tall boy clasping the pommel, tipped forward like a jockey entering the stretch. We were chasing the horizon through folds of ancient mountain, speeding past rickety soda stands, half-acre fields, stunted cactus, and giant rocks painted with names of political candidates and football teams and religious slogans: *¡VAYA CON DIOS!*

Children backed off, then waved, sometimes scampering alongside before being left in the dust — that limitless dust of the Sierra Madre. When I glanced toward your son his face was intent, eyes half shut against the sun and grit while the creature between his legs bolted over a ditch. Had you ever seen him like this, in such a rapture of concentration and pure, wordless fear? His pony, named Zorro, sideswiped a tree, and Kip laughed aloud in terror, then slung himself to one side, sawing at the reins. Then it hit me the boy could be thrown, that he was, as was I, inches from disaster. I thought of Geraldo, hung up on the cactus; people did die here. My heart quickened. I saw how it would be: Kip floating slow motion over the pony's head and landing with a soft thud on the ground. I would leap from my own pony and be at his side in seconds, hands cradling his cracked head, bending my ear to his mouth.

"What, Simone? What did he say?"

It was you, tugging at my shirt, begging to hear it again.

For I possessed his final minutes in this world, and over and over you would beg me to tell it again, scraping for details: "Could he see? Was there any pain?"

These ponies were sure-footed and completely disobedient. They raced to a spot near the lake where they stopped, flanks quivering, long enough to graze on the lush grasses. There was an overpowering stench of rotting fish and the bushes were laced with yards of toilet paper and used diapers. Underneath my thighs, the animal's belly swelled as she chewed, then swallowed.

You suggest a drink in the airport lounge and, checking her watch, she agrees. When you pull out a chair at one of the little tables by the window she says no and strides toward the bar. Where you yearn for privacy, she wants only to avoid it.

She drinks gin and chatters about people you don't care about. You notice the way men look at her; that crew of Hong Kong businessmen in their perfectly tailored tan suits can't keep their eyes off her. She swings one leg over the other and twirls around once on the stool. Your throat goes dry. For once, you can't think of a thing to say.

Kip reached down to knock a pebble out of his sneaker, then tipped his foot back into the shoe. We'd handed the horses back to Señor Fernandez at the *rancho* on the edge of town, and now we were clomping stiffly up the highway. The boy walked a few paces ahead. He'd pulled off his shirt and knotted it around his waist. His shoulders were thin, like a child's, and he moved with a bowlegged stride, the horse still under him. Somewhere during the ride he'd lost his hat, and now he kept batting at his hair and muttering curses when it fell over his face. When I bumped into his side once to avoid a careening motorbike, he leapt away. He swung his whole body as he walked, poking his hands in and out of his pockets as if he couldn't decide which was more comfortable. I tried to see what would be the man in him — that cocky sway of hips, or the jerky leap to safety?

"That's my flight." She's tilting her head, listening to the crackle of loudspeaker.

"There's plenty of time." You lift a hand to order another drink but she's already sliding off the stool. "What's the rush?"

She gives you a look full of weariness and pity.

I edged closer. "What's your mother's boyfriend like?" I'd already heard your version, that he was eight years her junior, Russian émigré.

"She gets off on that," you'd said, "the Cossack thing. Doesn't notice he's an idiot when he talks in that Pushkin accent."

Kip slowed down a fraction. "Vlad? He's all right."

"Does he live with you?"

"Sort of."

I pressed on. "Is it hard seeing your mother with a new man?"

"Not really."

We were walking side by side now, but with three or four feet between us. Whenever I got closer, he'd angle off toward the ditch, keeping the space constant.

"Why do you suppose she did it?"

Kip glanced at me and gave a little smile. "Because my old man kept screwing his students."

I let out a sound, but it disappeared into the racket of a bus that tore around the corner, dangling passengers from the rear door. A cloud of dust and exhaust coated us head to toe.

"He's one of those, is he," I said at last, in a voice that fought to sound knowing. I touched my throat with my fingers; suddenly it was hard to swallow.

"Every time when she finds out, he gets sorry."

"Right," I said, as if I knew this was the pattern in such cases.

"Calls Mom at work every hour."

I nodded. *Men* — and remembered the way Adela loaded the word, adding a conspiratorial squeeze.

Kip let me catch up.

"Every fucking day he calls, since he left town." His voice had a curious sing-song quality. He was enjoying this, I realized.

"Soon as the rates go down .... *rring!* Guess who? My old man shouting through some crackly phone, people jabbering away in Spanish."

"He's been calling from Mexico?" My hands clenched, still yanking at the reins.

Kip gave me a queer look. "Why do you think we're here?"

I was torn between not wanting to sound like a fool, and needing to know.

"He called you?"

"Every day." Kip lifted his leg to crush a Coke can. Then he put on a whiny voice I realized was meant to be yours: *"Please, I need my family ..."*

With those few words, everything changed. Of course. I thought about those times you'd disappear and I'd wonder where you'd gone. Snuck into the *larga distancia*, that hole in the wall where you line up to use the one ancient phone, where the girl sits at a table making the connection, shouting into the receiver, then collects money in a metal box. Must have set you back a peso or two. When you'd come back to the house I'd feel something, that I had to wave my hands in the air — yoo-hoo, anyone home?

What about the evening I ran into you on a side street and your face was crumpled, and I was sure you'd been crying?

"You okay?" I put a hand on your wrist.

"Sure," you answered, and accepted my smile of relief.

Yet I'd wondered for days. Weeks.

Or what about those times you'd pace around the house for half an hour, even longer, before scooping up your wallet and muttering, "I'm going to town." No explanation. Is that how it was for you, Otto, each day framed around the necessary phone call? And did you fall into bed each night hoping one desire would push clear the other?

ONLY TICKET HOLDERS BEYOND THIS POINT.

She's leaving you inch by inch, second by second, pushing through the heavy glass doors toward the metal detector and conveyor belt. She makes a half-turn.

"Take good care of him, Otto."

This isn't what you want to talk about. She poses, one hip jutted out, in her dark tailored suit with the short skirt. She's breathing quickly. So are you. You reach out but she pulls away, irritated. She hates it when you do that. The door begins to close slowly. You are the man she fell in love with, you want to cry out. With your black T-shirt and khakis, arms crossed in front of your chest, hair cropped short, a massive painting behind ... but she's forgotten. She doesn't see this any more. She sees an aging fool who chases his students, spending endless nights at the local pub, sliding one elbow through sticky beer to whisper in some girl's ear, "Care to come back to my studio?" She sees this chin covered with gray stubble and a face crumpled with pain; she sees a man who can't stand to lose. You know all this: you read it in her face, which has an eager, excited look. You feel incredibly horny. You want to hike up her skirt at the edge of Departure Lounge number 32 and fuck her under the nose of the sleepy-eyed security guard with the rifle tucked between his legs. You want to be inside her this instant, and she knows it. She gives a little laugh as the door finally closes with a swish of displaced air. You watch as she marches through the security envelope, dropping her satchel onto the moving belt. You watch with a glimmer of hope while some dark-eyed kid in a faded uniform peers through the X-ray at your wife's underwear and toilet kit. Why didn't you think to drop something in there — a joint, or some antiquity: one of those pre-Columbian figurines. There are strict laws about smuggling out heritage objects.

Handcuffs. Cries of indignation and fear. Her twisting body freezes and she is staring at you, pleading, "Help me, Otto."

There wasn't a hint of color in your face; you looked whacked out, exhausted. If I touch him, I thought, he'll crumble, like those clay figures they pull from tombs, sealed off from air for centuries only to decay with a single human touch.

"Kip told you this?" you said in a weary voice.

"Yes." I'd waited up till dawn for your return.

"It's true," you said finally. "I did do that. I did call, as often as I could."

"But why —"

"Why?" Suddenly you didn't sound sleepy. "Because I had to."

"And what about those other students." My own voice was thick with fatigue. "Am I the latest in a long line?"

"Don't do this to yourself."

"To myself?" I gave a strained laugh. I'd spent hours on the icy veranda, sipping sticky-sweet Kahlúa in coffee, waiting for this moment.

You leaned over to tug your boots off. "I wanted this to work, you have to believe me. I thought I could sidestep my real life, keep goosing the dream."

"The dream?" My voice rose. "I thought I'd finally entered my real life!"

"I know it." You held out a hand, which I ignored.

"You tell me over and over to "see what's there," not what I think should be there, or was there the last time I looked. Not to be trapped by habits of seeing. I believed all that, Otto!" A shiver of self-righteousness flew through my body. "This isn't just a moral betrayal — it's aesthetic. I've been conned from day one!"

You rose to your feet. "How far were you willing to go, Simone? After you got what you wanted from me? A year? Maybe two? What about when you'd skimmed the goods, then what? I'm forty-five years old."

"What does that have to do with it?"

"Everything. I'm sorry: you want a scene but I can't do it. It's been a long and immensely difficult day."

"How do you think —" I stopped. "Where am I in all this?"

We were both silent for several seconds.

"I wish I knew, Simone."

"That's not good enough."

You opened your palms. "What can I say, but this is what you get: this is who I am — a beat old man."

"You're not old!"

"Well, old is how I feel, dear." Then you walked right past me, through the courtyard, and ducked into the kitchen. Without bothering to turn on the light you opened the fridge door and pulled out a beer.

Then nothing.

You must be standing in the dark, drinking. If I wanted more I'd have to follow you in there. I smelled burning rubber coming from somewhere in the hills. It was a heavy, pointless smell; teenagers dragging tires into a pile, then lighting them for kicks. You didn't look up when I entered, but said in a flat tone, "It isn't going to get any better, is it?"

"What do you mean?" I couldn't hide the chill in my voice.

You reached into your jacket pocket and pulled out a small folder.

"I have something for you."

Even in the dark I recognized the logo of Canadian Airlines.

"I'm so sorry." You held the packet out and waited for me to take it. "I thought I wanted you here. I was wrong."

☀ 20 ☀

THERE WERE SIX days before my flight. Our bodies became sealed in separate envelopes. You rarely looked at me, and never touched me except by accident. When you needed to speak you would tilt your head like someone who was hard of hearing. You were determinedly correct in a new way, holding doors open or asking did I prefer white meat or dark. I thought of Emily Dickinson: "After great pain, a formal feeling comes ..."

When I stretched my legs under the table and happened to brush yours, you hastily jerked away.

You ignored my hungry stare. My eyes followed as you walked from one part of the room to another, picking up a book or switching a light on, and I knew by the measured way you moved that you felt me watching. You slipped the pen from your shirt pocket, uncapped it, and began to draw, letting nothing stop you from making your marks on the page.

You shrank from my touch because you thought I might misread it. You knew how I jumped to interpret the most innocent gesture in a favorable way. I began to devise a plan; I must neutralize myself, show how I fully accepted the switch in our relationship. I had to make you feel safe, for I could not endure days more of this.

I came up behind your back as you stood staring out at the valley. You had tried to interest your son in a game of chess. He'd lasted for a dozen moves before yawning, "It's so *slow*" — and then there'd been an argument. The scene ended with Kip dropping back into the hammock and you striding over to the window.

I put my hand lightly on your waist.

You stiffened.

"It's okay," I said, "we can still be friends."

I heard air escape from your mouth; you must have been holding it in for days.

"I'm not upset," I said.

You spun around. "Really?"

I nodded.

"I've been feeling so crummy," you said.

"I know."

"I hated hurting you."

I nodded again.

"We *are* friends, dammit." You pulled me into your chest and I heard the welcome thump of your heart.

After this, we touched often. Even in front of your son you freely reached for me, slinging an arm around my waist or shoulder, and once even planted a kiss on my mouth. I was neutralized. Safe. You thought.

"You awake in there?"

"Sure." I lifted myself up on one elbow and strained to see. I'd heard Mother's footsteps on the creaky pine floor and listened to whispers and the soft scrape of cupboard doors opening and shutting.

"I'm off. Your father will drive me down to the bus." Then she leaned over the bed and found my forehead in the pitch black of pre-dawn.

Aunt Amy had had an operation, something to do with her "female parts," and Mother was heading for the prairie to help out and offer what she called "moral support and a shoulder to cry on."

"How long will you be?" Father asked in a strange, quiet voice when he heard the news.

"Depends on how it goes, how quickly she recovers."

I could see he was fighting with himself, making little noises in his throat before he finally said, "Do you have to go?"

She seemed to expect this question and her face tightened. I heard myself answer, "Of course she must go; it's her sister."

What was he scared of? That the plane would crash? No, I decided, it was something even more frightening. He was scared she'd find something out there, perhaps just a smell, or an interesting sound, and she would stride off in that familiar distracted way, and forget all about us.

Bob's baggy shorts gaped when he let his legs fall open. He was so thin, like the men in the sepia photos in Father's leather-bound copy of *Colonial Explorers*, gaunt but smiling, as they emerge from the Amazonian jungle. He even wore the right kind of hat, a ratty sombrero, crushed and stained.

"My God, this thing is slow!" I shouted over the sound of the ancient motor.

We were chugging along in a *lancha* toward the far shore of the lake to a settlement called Dos Cumbres. Kip was perched on the gunwale, hair streaming in front of his face, as Don Eduardo, the fisherman we'd hired for the day, steered into the wind.

I was drunk. So was your son. So, it goes without saying, was Bob.

"Give the boy another hit," Bob said, tossing the flask.

My plane left in two days. Every second had become laced with meaning; I no longer had the discipline to behave well; I didn't even try. I'd been stalking you, shadowing your every move, to the point where I'd perch on the rim of the tub as you shaved. It wasn't too late to make you change your mind. When you swallowed the food I prepared, I watched your throat and imagined the journey of beans through esophagus to belly. You bore up to this attention with steely indifference; you simply went about your business, stepping around me when necessary.

"Who wants to go out on the lake?" Bob had appeared at our door the night before in his undershirt and khakis.

"Not me," you said quickly. "But take these two — they need an outing."

"I'm leaving in two and a half days!" I protested, and I could have been much more exact. Time was precious, shaved off in seconds.

"All the more reason to get in some sightseeing." You leaned into my ear and whispered. "Bob is a sad fellow now; he needs company."

Since when did you care about Bob?

Don Eduardo slowed as we entered a weedy patch, and lifted the motor. The propeller was draped with green sludge. Half the lake was clogged with reeds. We'd left San Pat behind, its long wooden wharf jutting out, seeded with car tires.

"This is what comes out your tap," Bob announced cheerfully, trailing his finger in the water. "Nail a piece of rusty screen over the intake pipe and pump the muck into town. Keeps out the solid wastes, dears, the diapers and sawed-off limbs and floating rats — the rest sifts into your *sopa*." He eyed Kip. "What do you reckon this boy is thinking of?"

Kip hadn't said a word since we pushed off.

Something got into me.

"He's brooding about his girlfriend."

Kip glowered.

"Do you have a girlfriend?" I persisted. "Bet they can't keep their hands off you back home." Then I reached out and touched your son's knee. He gripped the underside of the gunwale with his fingertips. Above, the ripped awning was flapping like crazy.

"Full speed ahead, Don Eduardo!" Bob cackled as the ancient motor putt-putted through the weedy lake.

It isn't going to get any better, is it?

Kip's leg stiffened, he shifted weight and started drinking way too fast, chugging tequila as if it were soda pop. I should do something, slow the kid down. His cheeks were flushed an unhealthy red.

I thought I wanted you here ...

Kip belched, then wiped his mouth. From the other side of the boat Bob laughed.

"Maybe he's got a *boy*friend."

"Fuck I do," Kip muttered.

"He speaks!" Bob's eyes widened, then, bored of the game, he hoisted himself up. "Know what this little trip is about? Today is Geraldo's funeral."

I twisted around. "At Dos Cumbres?"

"No. Back in San Pat. Which is why I had to get the fuck out. When they go back to Mama's for a *copacita* some cousin's going to get raging drunk and yell, 'Where's that faggot who hauled off our angel boy?'" Bob cocked an imaginary pistol and pressed it to his temple.

"They'd shoot you?"

"You bet, dear."

I stared at the approaching shore where a woman was dragging laundry back and forth through the water.

"What if they find out where you've gone?"

"Then we're in deep shit, girl."

We.

"Of course we may never get there," Bob went on. "Look at this crate. See a single lifejacket? How many leaks you figger old Don Eduardo's stuffed with putty and chewing tobacco? Every year they lose one of these tubs — this isn't O Canada, dear."

I let my hand slide off Kip's knee. Why did I ever imagine I was safe?

There was a tiny splash, so undramatic I barely noticed it over the motor sound. But when the boat suddenly heaved, sending the empty flask tumbling under my feet, I let out a shriek.

"I'll be damned," Bob said. He was pointing over my shoulder.

Following the direction of his finger I stared toward the now unobstructed gunwale where Kip had been perching a few seconds earlier.

"Cut the motor!"

Don Eduardo already had, and his face, which till now had been impassive, became animated. "*¡El joven!*" he cried, and quickly brought the boat around.

"Why the hell did he do a damn fool thing like that?" Bob said.

"Where is he?" I was searching madly over both sides of the boat. "Did he fall? Jump?"

Bob nodded toward the foredeck. His chunky sneakers lay there, no socks. I grabbed them and darted back toward the side. There was nothing to look at; the water seemed to have swallowed the boy without a trace. Where he'd been sitting a dragonfly sunned its wings.

"He'll pop up soon, dear," Bob said, fanning himself with his hat. "He's a floater, that one."

The bow moved slowly, cutting into a tight circle, pushing aside corpses of tiny silvery fish. From the dock we heard excited shouts. Any moment the skin of water would part and the boy would shoot up laughing, spouting a fountain of water. That's what they did back home after diving. Just when I thought they'd been under forever — up they came, hair plastered to their skulls.

"*¡Por allí!*" Don Eduardo was pointing to a spot off the port bow. At first I saw nothing. Then a commotion of arms and the plaintive yell, "Help!"

"What did you do?" Your fingers dug into my wrist.

I began to improvise quickly. "I kept my eyes pinned to the spot —"

"Good!"

"Chucked my sandals."

You nodded. "The fucker can swim; he got his bronze medal when he was twelve."

Maybe so, I thought, remembering the way he'd slugged tequila. Of course you didn't know that part.

"What did you do?"

"Dove in, of course."

"But you can't swim, Simone."

"I had to, didn't I?"

A brief, admiring look. "What about Bob?"

I snorted. "Conked out on the floor of the boat."

"So you dove —" The fingers ground into my wrist.

"And paddled over — he hadn't gone completely under —"

"And?"

Suddenly I knew how it went. "I felt around for him. He was slippery, but I got his chin and lifted it so he could breathe—"

"Yes!"

"— dog-paddled back to the boat."

"Which was?"

"No more than a dozen feet away."

"They hauled you in —"

"Hauled us both in and —"

"How long?" you said.

"How long?"

"From beginning to end. From when he dumped to the moment when you got his chin up?"

"Jeez, Otto, I don't know." I caught your expression and added quickly: "Couldn't have been more than a few minutes."

"A few? Three? Ten?"

"No more than three — tops."

Your grip lightened. I looked down and saw four white crescents tattooed to my wrist.

"Thank you," you said at last.

I nodded, waiting.

"Simone?"

"Yes?"

"Please stay."

Early food-chain inhabitants clung to the bow and the skin of my forearm as I dipped in. The abrupt break from motor sounds was luminous, like when your ears pop and the world is full of sharp, subtle noises. On the dock a small girl stared toward us with an expression of calm interest. She was wearing a Toronto Blue Jays cap, several sizes too big, and a flowered dress. Lazily, without lowering her gaze, she reached for a naked toddler who was lunging toward the edge.

The trouble was, Otto, I couldn't see bottom. I've always hated that.

My chest pressed against the gunwale: where the hell was he? The water was a murky green, littered with dead fish and algae.

Isn't this what I'd wanted? Hadn't I imagined this moment from the second we pushed off?

Please stay.

Suddenly a set of white fingernails gripped the side of the boat and we pitched abruptly to starboard. A geyser of water shot into the air, then Kip's head rose, hair plastered to his forehead.

"Too bad," Bob said, clutching my arm for balance. "That pretty swan dive will have to wait."

He knew exactly what I'd been thinking, the heroic rescue, your frantic demand for details. I reached out with both arms and hauled the boy in.

☀ 21 ☀

FATHER WAS CONKED out on the beach with a scruffy gray towel draped over his chest and face to prevent sunburn. He was years ahead of the doctors, wary of UV rays and reflected light. The newspaper, folded to the crossword puzzle, lay held down by a beige Hush Puppie. A Thermos of rosehip tea was buried in the sand up to its neck. That was for later, when he would awaken, thirsty and cracked-lipped. It was Saturday so the transistor radio was tuned to the Metropolitan Opera.

I was in the water deeper than usual, picking my way over the rocky bottom, eyes fixed to the cliff that rose on the other side of the inlet. The boys were stripped to their shorts, playing chicken. They'd pretend to be unaware they were nearing the edge, then when the ground broke beneath they'd let out wild yells and for a split second would hover, arms windmilling like cartoon characters expecting to helicopter back to safety.

"Idiots," Father had muttered, giving them a quick glance before dropping to the sand. "Check the lowered brows and oversize ears."

A muscular boy with a long torso stood on the cliff waiting his turn. He peered across the teardrop-shaped bay and waved — at me. Who else was there to wave at? Two arms crisscrossed the sky like windshield wipers. I returned the wave, then dropped backwards into the water and felt my legs rise. Was he watching? I thought so. His gaze was warm and blank, like the sun. I floated effortlessly, sculling with my hands, and saw my feet stick up like twin rudders.

We stood under the clock in the little terminal building, a concrete bunker with bright plastic chairs and a gleaming floor.

"You'll have a stopover in Mexico City."

"Right."

"Stick close to your luggage."

I nodded. How did this happen? How did I get here?

"You'll need more pesos." You dug into your pockets. My purse was already bulging. "Really, Otto, I think —"

"There's airport departure tax." Another fistful of bills was pressed into my palm. Then you checked your watch, coordinating it with the digital clock above. We were both edgy, hardly looking at each other. The waiting room held half a dozen passengers, men in crisp suits heading for business in the capital. A shoeshine boy worked his way through them, kicking his wooden box along the floor.

You looked out of place in your worn jeans and wrinkled shirt. You were taller than anyone here by half a dozen inches, and hadn't shaved in days.

"You'll get into Toronto by supper. There's someone you can bunk with?"

"My Dad's cousin Louie."

How could I stop this?

You sucked deeply at a cigarette and twisted it 180 degrees. The loudspeaker crackled and an ancient commuter plane taxied toward us on the tarmac. I could see the pilot high in the window, reaching to adjust some control. He wore, reassuringly, ornate epaulets and a captain's hat.

Your hand clenched over mine and you nodded toward the uniformed woman who was walking briskly to the exit. The businessmen folded their newspapers, hefted their shoulder bags, and began to follow her. The stench of diesel fuel swept through the air, along with the low rumbling of engine noise. Beyond the runway, brown mountains swelled toward the rising sun. It was early, and still so cold we could see the breath of the mechanic as he flagged the pilot in closer. The fuel smell grew stronger, and the noise became so loud the glass panes of the terminal building began to shudder. Soon I'd be strapped into that ancient aircraft, eyes pressed to the window, while you bounced back toward the truck, back to your life.

"Let me take that." You lifted my suitcase and pushed toward the exit. The back pocket of your jeans was torn, revealing a dark oblong of unweathered denim.

For a heady instant I thought, He's coming with me! Until I realized you were just trying to hurry things along.

When I'd mounted the metal stairs you passed the bag up and looked straight into my face.

"Goodbye, Simone."

"I guess this is it." The other passengers squeezed by, flattening me against the railing. Seconds to go. It wasn't too late. You could still speak the words I ached to hear. We'd jump back into the truck, laughing at how close it had been.

You reached for your cigarette and tossed it to the ground, saying something in a low voice.

"What?" I leaned over eagerly.

For a moment I thought you wouldn't answer. The flight attendant touched my shoulder. "*¿Señorita?*"

I shrugged her off. "What?" I insisted.

You stepped backwards, glancing toward the parking lot. "I told myself," you said, "that once I got you safely packed away on the plane I'd quit smoking forever."

☀ *22* ☀

"I'M AT WONG'S!" Mother shouted. The line was terrible.

Wong's was the restaurant in Rupert where we made phone calls.

"Can you hear me?"

"Just." I reached over to shut the window as a streetcar rumbled by. "What are you doing home?"

It was a Wednesday and all that year she'd spent weekdays in Toronto, working on her master's in Italian studies at U of T, going back to the cabin only on weekends.

"Something's wrong with your father."

"What do you mean?"

"He won't eat."

I relaxed. "You know why; he feels deserted, and he'll prove it by half starving himself. Don't give in, Mom." I was facing a poster from a Francis Bacon exhibition: "The Screaming Pope." This was a friend's loft I was renting, right across from the Queen Street Mental Health Center. I'd been back in Canada two and a half years.

"First he decided he can't have yeast so I bake Boston

brown bread, then he's off dairy products and fruit because they give him gas. This week it's no salt or carbohydrates. I leave food wrapped and labeled, and on the weekend when I come home it's gone rotten."

We still had the old-fashioned wooden icebox. Things didn't keep forever.

I heard the clash of steel cutlery in the background: no one in Rupert used chopsticks.

"Don't let him rope you in," I advised. "He's threatened by your newfound freedom, your forays into the larger world." Encouraged by her silence, I went on. "One of these mornings he'll wake up and fry himself a dozen eggs."

"He's down to sunflower seeds, Simone. The shells are everywhere."

Father had inoperable pancreatic cancer. When I saw him on the bed at the Rupert Regional Hospital I actually didn't recognize him for several seconds.

He'd shrunk. One arm lay like a weathered twig on top of the blanket, taped to an IV needle. The hump under the bedclothes was tiny, like a child's body. His face, when I first walked in, was absolutely still. He was gazing at the ceiling and slowly swung his eyes to where I stood.

"Simone, old thing," he said, brushing sunflower husks off his chest. "They tell me I have a bit of a problem."

I kissed his cheek, affecting a breezy style.

"Never thought I'd catch you in a place like this."

"It's not so bad."

This easy accommodation, so unlike him.

Mother waited outside the room, decked out in a crisp Jaeger blouse and stirrup pants. I could feel her listening, judging the moment to enter.

"Does it hurt, Dad?"

"Not so much." He indicated the plastic bag on top of the IV unit. "Know what's in there? Morphine. Your old man's turning into a junkie."

("Did you know there are two kinds of beriberi?" he asked once, looking up from the Harvard medical newsletter. "Wet beriberi and dry beriberi; the latter causes damage to the peripheral nerves ...")

I watched as he took short painful steps to the bathroom, pushing the IV trolley. The back of his gown was coming undone but he didn't seem to notice. He stopped for a moment, bending over and grimacing. "Damn!"

"Can I help?"

"No," he said firmly, "you can't."

Then I heard myself say, "Maybe we could look after you at home."

"You kidding?" He was panting. "Where would we plug this thing into? No, dear, I've been hauled, kicking and screaming, into the twentieth century."

The thing was, he didn't kick or scream. The terminal diagnosis seemed to give him a sort of grim satisfaction. Instead of raging against the dying of the light he embraced its process, as if he were finally proving some long-held thesis: the world really was a dangerous place. And, of course, he loaded up on facts. We were sent to the library, not for inspirational self-help books like *Living with Cancer*, but to cart back special inter-library loans: texts by doctors for doctors, full of photographs of diseased organs. He chattered about the minutiae of institutional life, the state of his blood pressure, white blood cell count, how many CC's of urine he'd passed that morning. Everything was charted and monitored. He looked forward to the comings and goings of specialists: endocrinologists and internists and oncologists who would begin by asking, "Are you comfortable, Mr. Paris?" My father, who had always despised authority, became extraordinarily deferential around these men and women in white coats; they were the holders — or withholders — of information, the Gods of Disease.

Yet he never spoke of death.

"Does he allow himself to think of it?" I said to Mother after an especially frustrating visit. I'd been reading Kübler-

Ross and the Tibetan Book of the Dead and was eager to share their wisdom. But all he wanted to talk about was something called "rates of absorption." He clung to facts, as if knowledge would save him. He genuinely found the role of enzymes in his deteriorating body of great interest.

"Heard of the islets of Langerhans?" he said, propping himself up with a wince of pain.

"You'll have to let him do this his own way," Mother said. The crisp blouse and stirrup pants were gone; she was back to wearing a flannel work shirt and dungarees.

When I opened my mouth to speak of spiritual matters a tight look came over his face. Sometimes I wondered if he surreptitiously reached for the call button, because it seemed that every time I ventured some thought about reincarnation or the dissolution of the ego, some nurse would bustle in and begin tugging the curtains around the bed.

"Would you step out for a few minutes, Miss Paris; we're going to give your father his bath."

"It's all ductwork," he called, just before the curtain sealed him off from sight.

I felt gypped. I wanted to hold cool compresses to his forehead, slip the straw between his lips, and massage his cold, rubbery feet. But he would have none of it.

"What do you think the nurses are paid for?"

"He doesn't want any change in the way we are with him," Mother said. "It would frighten him terribly."

"You take care of yourself," he said as I was leaving one evening. He'd slept a lot that day and had pushed away the lumps of mush that passed for food. "Ninety percent of road accidents occur less than five miles from home."

When I leaned over and kissed his eyelids they felt crispy, like parchment.

He died early that evening, listening to *Madama Butterfly* on the Walkman I'd bought him.

☀ *23* ☀

WHEN I GOT BACK to the cabin from the festival office in Rupert I checked the answering machine. Getting electricity and a phone line brought in was the first thing we did after Dad died. Then we went to Sears and bought a fridge, a washing machine, and a food processor. The only trouble was that the power was unreliable during storms or bouts of very cold weather, and whenever the lights suddenly flickered and dimmed, Mother and I would look knowingly at each other. We knew it was Dad's ghost, reminding us that technology must never lull us into complacency.

"Do you think the noise of the ship's motor will keep me awake?" Mother's voice sounded hyped-up on the tape; she was leaving in two days for a cruise to Alaska. There was a click, followed by a ringing, then her voice again: "Edie said I should take my own decaf ..."

I had to laugh. I'd given her an immersion heater on her last birthday. These days she was always on the go. Only last month she and a friend drove west to Vancouver Island, and now they were talking about buying into a bed-and-breakfast near Tofino. There was another series of rings followed by the click, then suddenly it was your voice, pitched so low and mock conversational, I quickly leaned to crank up the volume.

"Otto here." A long pause.

I realized I was still clutching my groceries.

"Nice seeing you the other day. I've got a proposal: why don't you drop by the studio? Say on Sunday. Brunch." You recited the address on Spadina Avenue. As if I didn't know, as if I hadn't slept with that boy with the shaved head just because his studio was in the same building.

Drop by. Toronto was a two-hour trip — yet you were so certain I'd come.

The torch, or flashlight, whatever it was, moved jerkily up the cliff path. At first I thought it was attached to a motorcycle, or one of those souped-up Jeeps the locals go in for. It was late, edging toward midnight, and I'd stepped out in the dark in my dressing gown to pee. I couldn't sleep, knowing I was going to see you.

The light came to rest at the top of the cliff. Then it lifted, as if grabbed, and I caught a glimpse of bicycle. Whoever it was balanced the lamp on the branches of the wind-torn maple, and then I saw a figure cross in front. Nicky, the boy who rode up every day at dusk. I recognized his stance; shoulders slightly bowed, hips swaying to work out the kinks. I drew my robe around my waist and tied the belt, without taking my eyes off him. He wasn't going to dive, not at this hour. Not when he couldn't see the pattern of rocks, catch the crest of the incoming wave.

The figure walked confidently to the edge of the cliff.

Boys this age do nutty things. They crave drama and disregard consequence. He'd probably come from some party where he'd been knocking back Budweisers. Maybe some girl laughed in his face, "Get real, Peel!" and hiked her blouse together. I stepped forward, feeling damp grass part against my calves. I should do something, yell a warning. I could blaze up there in a minute and a half. I listened hard, waiting for the tiny, telling splash. I pictured how it would be — my toes curling around the edge of the cliff, the suck of air — and the snap of cold as my body hit water.

"Cut!"

It was your voice, Otto, clear as the night air.
"Very corny, and face it, dear, you'd sink like a stone."

☀ 24 ☀

YOUR BUILDING HAD a belt-making factory on the ground floor, and as I pulled open the heavy glass door the smell of leather and dyes was overwhelming. I stepped over a pile of flyers advertising warehouse specials from places like Suzie's Frocks and Spadina Fur and Fashion. There was a row of old-style copper mailboxes on the wall, and down the corridor I spied the open door of the factory, machines chugging, even on Sunday. The place seemed brighter, and I decided it had been painted since I was last here, with the bicycle courier. I'd met him at a poetry event, and when he told me where he lived I felt myself tighten with interest. The fluorescents flickered then too, making the corridor shiver and change shape.

I hiked up the strap of my bag, which had been sawing a groove into one shoulder, and swapped sides. In it was a carton of wild raspberries, inadequately wrapped, and when I unzipped the top of the bag and peered in, I saw that the insides had become drenched with red juice.

"Up the stairs and take a left. My name's on the door."

I followed these instructions, clumping up two levels, past muffled sounds of music and machinery. Someone was playing drums, sweeping the high hat with a brush. I'd lived in places like this, with the same mix of smells: paint thinner, stale beer, and fried chicken.

On your door was, as promised, your name, printed on a piece of glossy paper and attached with two thumbtacks. I touched it, guessing it had been snipped from an exhibition catalogue. I was pretty sure I recognized the typeface from that show in Montreal: "The New Abstraction." Not so new now, Otto.

I was panting, as if I'd climbed a dozen sets of stairs, not just two.

So knock. Go in.

Not just yet. I set my ear to the door and listened, catching my breath. I wanted no heaving chest, no clatter of heartbeat. My ear sucked in a low rumbling noise, which opened up to voices, pitched deep.

"Coward!" I muttered. You didn't have the guts to take me on solo. Lay in some ballast, fill the chairs with warm bodies.

I knocked hard.

"It's open."

There was no handle, just a latch, which I lifted, then pressed forward. I stared across a vast sunny loft to where you were leaning over a counter, unplugging the kettle. There was a clang of cymbals and long low moans, which I quickly realized were coming from wall speakers.

"Tibetan monks," you called, beckoning me in. The voices rose, not together but staggered, one taking up when the other stopped. "Listen to those suckers!" you grinned, "resonating from their toes to their nose hairs!"

"Good morning, Otto."

You wiped your palms against your shorts. That's all you were wearing: straw thongs on your feet, a red bandanna on your head, and a pair of baggy blue shorts. I could see the line of white skin where the waistband sagged. You crossed the floor, never taking your eyes off me, and hesitated a few inches away.

"Still easy on the eye."

A trace of the old discomfort made me clench my bag.
I felt dampness against my hip —the leaking berries.

You wrapped both arms around my waist and my
mouth automatically slid into that dish at the base of your
throat. A hint of Ivory soap; you'd always scorned aftershave.
I broke away. "Is there coffee?"

"Sure." Your arms hung in the air.

One wall was entirely windows, most of them
propped open. I peered out into the nearly empty parking lot
below, then, scanning southeast, saw the bulge of SkyDome.
Further south the blue of the lake was dotted with white sails,
clumped together, as if in a regatta. The sun glared off the
water, forcing me to squint, and when I pulled my head back
inside, the loft seemed, for a moment, very dark and cool.

"Here's your coffee." You held out a mug filled to the brim.

We ended up eating brunch in the studio area, where
I helped arrange plates of croissants, sliced pineapples, and
raspberries over the drafting table.

"I want to show you a few things," you said, ripping
off several squares of paper towel to use as napkins.

I guessed it was because the idea of sitting down at a
regular table to eat made you nervous. Far easier to have a
topic, something to look at apart from each other.

You poured generous slugs of brandy into our coffee
and propped the new work, still unframed, against the wall.

"I call them drawings."

They were big, maybe three feet across and two feet
high, and elegant in a severe, uncompromising way.
Geometric shapes and bits of collage material floated across a
partly erased grid.

"What do you think?"

Half a dozen years ago I would have waited for clues,
to hear what you said before venturing my own opinion —
which I would deftly shape to match yours. I would have
listened to your tone and strived to imitate it. But this time I
looked through eyes that had been around. There had been
other authoritative voices, opinions that contradicted yours.

"I like this series best." I indicated four drawings that were more spread out than the others, less rigidly controlled.

You laughed.

"What's so funny?"

"I was just thinking they were dog shit."

The Tibetan gong clashed, the chanting ground to a halt, and I heard the swish of the CD mechanism.

"You're wrong, Otto. It's the others that are too tight, wrestled to the ground."

You looked startled, then reached into the Ace Bakery bag and pulled out a sticky bun. You took a bite, chewed thoughtfully, then said, "I know it."

I let out a breath.

You examined your cigarette, then stuffed the packet into your waistband. Suddenly I remembered.

"Didn't you quit those?"

"Funny thing, I just started up again last week."

I understood; that day when you visited me at the cabin.

A line of dark hair rode the ridge of your belly. My tongue had traced this path so many times and I remembered precisely the nubbly texture of skin, and the way your breath would grow long and deep, then suddenly quicken. Was this desire, or the memory of desire? When I looked up you were smiling, but in an edgy, uncertain way. You brushed the crumbs off the table into your cupped hand then popped them into your mouth. The drafting table divided us and I thought of all those early lessons in positive and negative space when you'd point out how the area around forms creates its own shape. "This is where the heat is!" you'd insist — and it was never the thing itself.

"How's the festival coming along?"

This was it, where you expected me to say, "Good news, you're on." Instead, I pretended to take the question literally.

"Terrific. I signed Randy Eggar for the drama studio."

"Eggar?" Your brow furrowed. "Don't know him."

"Are you serious? Randy's the hottest young director in town."

"Remember, Simone, I've been away."

Indeed. "For the media the big excitement has been about Sheila Bernstein, our visiting writer."

"Bernstein?" You lifted your shoulders and let them fall. "Sorry."

"*The Nice Girl*?" I waited for a sign of recognition. "*Pearl's Sinking Feeling*?"

"Afraid not."

"Well," I went on, "a community group is fighting her appointment tooth and nail —"

"Because ...?"

"The lesbian thing."

"Ah," you nodded, then laughed. "What do you expect from the folks up there. Bunch of pig farmers."

I stiffened. "In fact, they're not. The leaders of the group against Sheila are Maureen Chrichton who owns the jewelry store" — I couldn't believe I was defending the old bat — "and her husband Al, who's vice-principal at the district high school —"

"Say no more." You reached for coffee in the speckled camping pot. I guessed you hadn't bought a domestic appliance in twenty years. Your plates were chipped and mismatched, the mugs stained, and we shared a plastic spoon for stirring. Yet the art materials were in immaculate condition. Brushes leaned in jars, each tip swept to a point. Knives and tools were meticulously slotted on wall planks. Massive hanging shelves held canvases and drawings, all chronologically dated. The bookshelves were gunmetal gray, and I spotted fat exhibition catalogues dating back to the late sixties.

Yet, I realized, there was something missing.

"Where do you sleep, Otto?"

You pointed to the corner where a sleeping bag lay rolled up, and on top of it, one of those thin blue camping mats.

"All anyone needs." You affected a careless tone, as if sleeping were another tedious human necessity, like going to the bathroom, or daily flossing. You opened your mouth to speak again but were interrupted by the chop of a helicopter passing low overhead. We both glanced toward the window in time to see the tail disappear behind a bank tower. Whisking a desperately ill child to Sick Kids Hospital, I thought, or possibly a freshly harvested organ for transplantation. I'd once ridden the bus coming down from Rupert and had seen on the floor by the driver an orange picnic cooler with a sticker warning FRAGILE: CONTAINS HUMAN EYES.

"So then," you said, straightening, "your festival is in good hands."

"I hope so."

"Nice to get a younger crowd."

I nodded, but couldn't look at you. Instead my eye wandered to a shelf where I spotted the only visible souvenir of your six years in Mexico: a cream-colored pot with black markings. I remembered the exact day and place where you got it: Tzintzuntzan, a tiny village two hours' drive from San Patricio. We'd scurried around the Indian ruins for an hour, then headed into town for lunch. The restaurant you chose was tiny, furnished with three metal card tables and matching chairs, each emblazoned with the Pepsi logo. When our meal arrived, you exclaimed over the heavy clay plates. "I hate pottery, but these I love." So after eating we raced to the market before it closed and it was this wide-hipped pot that you picked up and clutched under your arm for the rest of the day.

"For teaching," you said, "fresh blood is vital. Old farts are always trapped in the past."

You were letting me off the hook, yet I felt no sense of victory or relief. I *could* hire you. Not for the full two months, but something smaller, more condensed. You could drive up for the weekend panel on "Producing Art in a Multi cultural Context" and zip home the next day ...

"Carmen called last night." You hiked up your shorts, let go, and they dropped immediately back over your hips.

"To tell me what an asshole I am — as if I needed reminding. She claims I'm fucking the kid up even worse. My very presence sets him off. Every time he sees me he acts out, because, she says, of his deep anger. 'Face, it Otto,' she says, 'you had your chance and you screwed up.'"

You stared at me with a look of bewilderment. "She *hates* me."

There were sounds out in the hallway of something heavy being dragged. The freight elevator thumped as it landed, and somebody cursed in Portuguese.

"*He* hates me." You lifted your arms and your shorts slumped another notch. "How do such things happen?"

Our eyes met, and something in me that had been clamped tight as a fist fell open.

"I'm sorry," I said.

You reached for the coffee mug but your hand was shaking like crazy.

"Shit." You took a breath and started again.

It was, if anything, worse this time. But you persisted, then finally set your lips against the rim.

"Look what you're doing to me, Simone."

You were scared; isn't this what I wanted?

"Look what you're doing to me," you repeated.

All I had to do was take a step forward to where you waited, every cell stippled with longing. Yet I was looking at you, seized not with desire but with interest. I was watching the intricate pattern of your face, the shadows on your sun-soaked skin, the way the blue of your shorts was picked up by the blue in a painting. I watched the way your body rose from the floor, and hovered there.

You set the mug down and took a step forward. Your face softened, suddenly without shadow.

"Well?" You lifted both hands, but as the silence stretched and I didn't respond, you let them drop back to your sides.

The edge of the drafting board nudged my back, then I heard the slow roll of a pencil before it fell to the ground.

"No," I said.

Such a small word, such a vast room.

You sucked in a breath and held it, and seemed to hang there in space, eyelids fluttering. I remembered how it felt to touch them that first time in class, when everything was expectation and desire. I remembered how under the thin membranes your eyes felt as fragile as baby birds.

ABOUT THE AUTHOR

ANN IRELAND is the author of *A Certain Mr. Takahashi*, which won the 1985 Seal First Novel Award. She received her B.F.A. from the University of British Columbia and has also studied at the Institute Allende in San Miguel de Allende. Ann teaches creative writing at Ryerson Polytechnic University. She lives in Toronto with her family.